She broke the silence between **"I have to admit, you are a pretty good dancer."**

"Pretty good?" He scoffed. "You haven't seen the half of what I can do."

Liam twirled Maya, pulled her in close, then dipped her, his face inches from hers as he held her in his arms. Her eyes widened in surprise. His gaze dropped to the little O her mouth formed as her breath came in short bursts. He returned his gaze to hers and slowly brought her vertical again, neither of them moving.

His heart pounded. There was something in her eyes. Something he couldn't explain. Liam pulled her closer and pressed his lips to hers. Maya went completely still, then slowly relaxed, slipping her arms around his waist beneath his suit jacket.

She tasted sweet and rich like a decadent dessert you couldn't get enough of but knew you would regret in the morning. His mind raced, wanting to taste her skin. To be enveloped in her scent.

Her kiss, raw and hungry, evoked a reaction from his body. He wanted her.

Dear Reader,

Welcome to the fictional North Carolina beach town of Pleasure Cove. The men of Pleasure Cove live hard and play harder. While they're willing to take risks in business and pleasure, past betrayals have rendered each man averse to risking his heart. Until he encounters the one woman he can't bear to walk away from.

The women of Pleasure Cove are smart, strong and independent. Each woman must overcome insecurities sowed in past relationships to discover that relinquishing control can be empowering and that the right man makes love worth the risk.

The series opens with a chance encounter between a divorced mom and a wealthy bachelor that leads to a sizzling summer and a future neither imagined.

Enjoy your visit with the men and women of Pleasure Cove. For series news, character insights, deleted scenes and more, visit reeseryan.com.

For your reading pleasure,

Reese Ryan

REESE RYAN

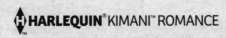

HARLEQUIN® KIMANI™ ROMANCE

Recycling programs
for this product may
not exist in your area.

ISBN-13: 978-0-373-86491-1

Playing with Desire

Copyright © 2017 by Roxanne Ravenel

For questions and comments about the quality of this book please contact us
at CustomerService@Harlequin.com.

Printed in U.S.A.

Reese Ryan writes sexy contemporary romance featuring colorful characters and sinfully sweet romance. She challenges her heroines with family and career drama, reformed bad boys, revealed secrets and the occasional identity crisis, but always rewards them with a well-earned happy ending.

A native of The Land (Cleveland, Ohio), Reese resides in North Carolina, where she carefully treads the line between being a Southerner and a Yankee, despite her insistence on calling soda "pop." She gauges her progress by the number of "bless your lil' hearts" she receives each week. She is currently down to two.

Reese is an avid reader with a to-be-read stack that resembles a small skyscraper, and a music lover with a serious thing for brilliant singer-songwriters and an incurable addiction to Broadway soundtracks and film scores. Connect with Reese via Instagram, Facebook or reeseryan.com.

Books by Reese Ryan

Harlequin Kimani Romance

Playing with Desire

This book is dedicated to my parents who inspired my love of reading, the English teachers who encouraged my interest in storytelling, my grandmother who was the very definition of a strong woman of color, my loving and supportive husband who taught me the value of persistence and organization, and my sweet and insightful son who continues to challenge and amaze me.

Acknowledgments

Thank you to everyone who has touched my life, career or this story in some way—big or small. My deepest gratitude to Keyla Hernandez for discovering my submission. Thank you to Keyla and editor Shannon Criss for helping me reshape the characters and create a stronger story. I am ever grateful for your guidance as we breathed new life into these characters who feel like old friends.

To my fabulous beta readers Lani Bennett, Jonetta Allen, Michelle Smith and Tonie Jones: thank you for your honest feedback and the precious investment of your time.

Thank you to Kianna Alexander and countless other current and former Heart of Carolina Romance Writers chapter mates who have inspired me with your struggles and successes, patiently answered my questions about the craft and business of writing, and shone light on the road ahead in this ever-changing business.

Chapter 1

Maya stepped inside Nadine's Seafood Restaurant. The first blast of frigid air from the restaurant was a welcome contrast to the hot, sticky sea air outside, but now a chill seeped into her skin.

She scanned the waiting lounge. Her half sister, Kendra, wasn't among the patrons waiting to be seated. Nor was she answering her cell. A knot tightened in Maya's belly. Kendra was a stickler for punctuality and her cell phone was practically an appendage.

Something isn't right.

Maya rubbed her arms, covered in goose bumps. She resisted the urge to adjust the strapless bodice of her dress. A birthday gift from Kendra, the thigh-skimming, baby-doll dress was shorter than anything she'd buy for herself. This was her last birthday as a twentysomething, so she'd agreed to wear it. After tonight, it would go to the back of her closet, where it belonged.

She was twenty-nine now and curvier than she'd ever

been. Five years of marriage, two beautiful daughters and a nasty divorce did that to a girl. Better to keep her imperfections under wraps.

"Hello, ma'am. Do you have a reservation for this evening?" The hostess's cheery voice dragged Maya out of her daze.

She cringed. Two hours of prep and makeup and she still couldn't avoid being called ma'am. "Yes. Under the name Kendra Williams, I think."

A frown formed on the hostess's thin lips. "Sorry, I don't have a reservation for Kendra Williams."

"Then it's under my name, Maya Alvarez."

"Ah…there you are." The hostess grinned. "Happy birthday to you, Ms. Alvarez. I'll seat you as soon as the rest of your party arrives. If you'd like to have a seat—" the girl gestured toward the bank of leather sofas beneath a window spanning the front of the restaurant "—or perhaps you'd prefer to wait at the bar."

Climb onto a bar stool in this dress? Not happening.

Maya thanked the girl, then surveyed the available seats. On one sofa, a sliver of space remained between two women chatting in what sounded like rapid-fire Chinese. An end seat remained on another where a couple was seated with a wailing infant.

The final sofa had a single occupant, a man wearing a charcoal-gray suit that fit his long, athletic frame like a well-designed glove. A patterned tie, in nearly the same deep shade of red as her dress, punctuated his crisp white shirt. One leg crossed over the other, the man stroked the neat beard that crawled along his strong jawline, connecting with a thin mustache. His deep tan hinted at long days spent at the beach, rather than in a tanning bed. The sides of his hair were cut low, but the crown had just enough length that it curled into dark, thick ringlets. She shivered at the brief sensation of running her fingers through them.

She licked her lips, a tingle crawling up her spine. The man glanced up, his penetrating gaze meeting hers. Maya's heart raced.

How long had she been gawking at him like an idiot?

The corners of his sensual mouth curled as he gave her a quick nod of acknowledgment.

Maya nodded in return and sank into the cushion at the opposite end of the leather couch. When she crossed her legs, the hem of her dress rose, exposing more of her brown skin, glistening with shimmering body oil. Uncrossing her legs, she tugged at the fabric and placed her small clutch in her lap.

Her spine stiffened. Aware of the man's stare, she glanced over at him. Lips curled into a lopsided smirk, he averted his gaze. Maya's cheeks flooded with heat. Two minutes exposed to in-the-flesh suit porn and she'd made a complete fool of herself. Twice.

The supple leather clung to her thighs as she leaned against the arm of the couch, maintaining maximum distance from the man.

"I don't bite." His velvety voice startled her. He had an accent. British, maybe. She hadn't expected that. Draping his arm over the back of the empty seat between them, he leaned closer. "Not usually, at least."

Maya stared at him with wide eyes. How the hell was she supposed to respond to an opening line like that?

The man's playful smile deepened.

"This seat taken?" An older man stood over them. His gaze shifted from Hot Suit Guy's face to hers before landing on her cleavage, enhanced by the strapless dress.

It figured that the one day she wasn't dressed in her usual soccer mom getup, she'd encounter a *viejo pervertido*—a dirty old man.

"No," they responded nearly simultaneously. The man's voice was reserved. Hers barely masked her disappointment. Their lack of enthusiasm didn't faze the ogler. He wedged his girth between them.

"Hello, beautiful." A lecherous grin slightly parted the older man's dry lips. "Dining alone tonight?"

Kendra's ringtone sounded from her clutch. *Perfect timing.* Maya forced a polite smile and held up one finger. Though not the one she wanted to hold up. She fished out her phone. "Hey. Everything okay?"

"Afraid not." Kendra heaved a sigh. "Honey, I can't make it tonight. Kai fell down the stairs after I dropped him off at my mom's. I had to turn around and take him to the hospital."

"Is he all right?" Maya pressed a hand to her chest.

"Knocked out his two front teeth. He needs stitches and emergency dental surgery. We're at the hospital now."

"Which one? I'll meet you there as soon as I can."

"Don't you dare." Kendra's tone was firm. "It's bad enough I'm bailing on you at the last minute. There's no way I'm letting you spend your birthday in the emergency room. You at the restaurant?"

"Yes." Maya turned her body away from the ogler's.

"Good. Dinner is still on me. Get the lobster, drinks, the works. I'll reimburse you. I feel so badly about this."

"I don't mind sitting with you guys, really. You've sat with me through worse."

"No. I'm serious, Maya. This is your first birthday without the girls since the divorce. I wanted to be there for you tonight."

Maya tugged her lower lip between her teeth. Her daughters were in Puerto Rico with their dad. Tomorrow afternoon they'd be flower girls when he wed the new and improved Mrs. Carlos Alvarez—a fresh-faced, barely legal coed. The one weekend of the summer his family church was available happened to be on her birthday weekend. She would never deny Sofia and Gabriella the chance to spend time with their dad. So she'd put on a brave face and watched them board a plane with their father two days ago. She'd been sulking ever since. "I miss them."

"I know, but they're going to have a blast spending the summer with their grandparents in Puerto Rico. Carlos is an asshole for choosing this weekend to get married, but he's given you a rare gift for a single mom. Time to yourself. Don't blow it. I need to live vicariously through you." They both laughed, then Kendra's tone turned somber. "Seriously, sis, promise me you'll have a good time tonight."

"I'll try." Maya bit back her disappointment and forced a smile into her voice, so Kendra wouldn't worry. Her daredevil nephew had given her sister enough to worry about tonight. She could certainly make it through one birthday solo. "Call me if you need something. Anything."

"We'll be fine. Now go have some fun. Flirt a little. Have the lobster. Then bring the bill back to me. That'll be my sorry-I-screwed-up-your-birthday gift. Love ya, babe." Kendra hung up before Maya could object.

Dinner for one tonight. Happy birthday to me.

Maya slid her phone back into her purse and looked up. A wolfish grin nearly split the old man's face. His eyes still drawn to her cleavage.

"Looks like you could use some company for dinner."

She gritted her teeth and swallowed the curses, most of them in Spanish, that came to mind.

"Mr. Westbrook, I'll seat you now." The hostess approached Hot Suit Guy with a menu.

"That's our table, love." The man stood, extending his hand to her.

Her eyes traveled up the sleeve of his expensive suit. *Definitely athletic cut.*

The man was tall, and even more handsome upon closer inspection. Michael Ealy meets Adam Levine handsome. Her heart beat a little faster and a jolt of electricity traveled the length of her spine. She shuddered inwardly. Handsome, charming and he damned well knew it.

A man like that is bad news.

She had two kids and a divorce decree to prove it. It would be safer to pass on the invitation. And she intended to, because that was just what she did. She made sensible choices. Played it safe. But the man's expectant grin taunted her. Dared her to venture beyond the cozy cocoon of her safe and predictable life.

He's being a gentleman. Why not let him?

Maya placed her hand in his and let him pull her to her feet. Heat radiated up her arm from the warmth of his hand on hers. His clean scent—like freshly-scrubbed man, new leather and sin—was captivating.

Maybe sin didn't have a scent, per se. But if it did, it would smell like him, with his mischievous smile and eyes so dark and intense they caused a flutter in her belly whenever she looked into them.

Tucking her hand into the bend of his elbow, he followed the hostess to their table. Maya concentrated on putting one foot in front of the other. The simple feat required all of her concentration.

"Thank you." The words tumbled from her lips the second the hostess left them alone. "It was kind of you to come to my rescue, but I doubt dinner with a random stranger was your plan for tonight. I'll order something to go from the bar and let you get back to your evening." The inflection at the end of the phrase indicated it was a question. She hadn't intended it to be. The thinking part of her brain clearly wasn't the part of her body in control at the moment.

His dark eyes glinted in the candlelight. "My motives aren't as altruistic as you might imagine. The opportunity to dine with a beautiful woman presented itself, so I seized it. I'd much prefer your company to eating alone."

Her heart pounded. Eating with a stranger would be uncomfortable. Dining alone on her birthday when there was a better option...that was just sad.

Maya surveyed the man. He was confident. Cocky even. And sexy as sin. There was that word again. She sighed. No point in denying the truth. His penetrating stare and impish grin stirred the kind of feelings that were a dangerous luxury she couldn't afford. Regardless of her body and brain going rogue, she had zero interest in anything more than an hour of dinner conversation with another adult.

They were in a restaurant full of people. What harm would there be in sharing a meal?

She furrowed her brows. "You really want to do this?"

"I do." His eyes twinkled with a mixture of amusement and disbelief. Fitting for a guy who probably wasn't accustomed to working this hard to get a woman to say *yes*.

"Then thank you for the dinner invitation, Mr. Westbrook."

He extended his large hand across the table. "Please, call me Liam."

Maya slipped her hand into his. She allowed herself a moment to revel in the heat of his firm grip. How would it feel to have those hands on her waist? Her hips? Her... Maya's cheeks warmed, and she withdrew her hand. "Pleased to meet you, Liam."

He smiled. "So, Ms. Alvarez...it is Ms., isn't it?" She nodded as she absently stroked her empty ring finger. The bareness still felt new. She'd only stopped wearing her wedding band six months earlier. When Carlos announced his engagement to what's-her-face. "What shall I call you?"

She raised her eyes to his again. "Maya."

"Well, happy birthday, Maya. Sorry you're stuck with me on your big day. Let's make the best of it, shall we?" He winked.

"Thank you." Maya exhaled, easing the tension in her

shoulders. Small talk. She could do small talk. "So, where are you from, Liam?"

"London, originally. Spent the past few years here in the US working in New York and then LA."

"What brings you to Pleasure Cove?"

There was a flash of something in his eyes. Anger? Or maybe pain? But it was quickly displaced by the luminous glint that was there before. "I'd planned to return to London earlier this year, but things change. So here I am."

"What do you do?"

"I'm in hospitality."

She should have known. Pleasure Cove, once a sleepy little fishing and beach town favored by old money snowbirds and retirees, had quickly become a playground for the upwardly mobile and nouveau riche. There were at least three new resorts and as many condos under construction. "Which hotel?"

"Pleasure Cove Luxury Resort."

"The crown jewel of Pleasure Cove," she said, echoing the ad. "I saw the renderings online. It's going to be unlike anything in Pleasure Cove."

"That's the plan." He tapped the table. "But that's enough about me. I want to hear all about you, birthday girl."

Maya was relieved when the server interrupted them. The woman introduced herself, set down two glasses of water and rattled off the specials.

Maya ordered, then quickly added, "Separate checks, please."

"I invited you to dine with me as my guest. Allow me to pay for your meal."

"I can't ask you to do that."

"You didn't, and I insist. Can't allow you to pay for your own birthday meal." He gave a mock shudder. "How uncivilized."

She held back a grin. "My sister couldn't make it tonight, but she's paying. So, if that's your concern, we're good." Maya shifted her gaze back to the server. "Separate checks, please."

"If that's what you really want." He gave her a conciliatory smile.

Maya nodded, relieved he'd given in so easily. She'd ordered steak and lobster. Best not to give Hot Suit Guy any ideas.

"I detect a faint accent, Maya. Are you native to Pleasure Cove?" Liam studied her.

Something about his gaze unnerved her. It penetrated her skin with a heat that trailed down her spine. "My mother is Cuban and speaks English with a heavy accent. My dad, who is African American, was a marine on active duty until I was about six. My maternal grandmother, who only spoke Spanish, lived with us, so my brother and I learned Spanish and English simultaneously. I'm fluent in both. I do have a slight accent, but mostly when—"

"You're nervous?" One side of his mouth curved, deepening the dimple in his right cheek. "Can't imagine why I'd make you nervous."

Another server decanted a bottle of wine, then poured a glass for each of them. Maya picked up her glass so fast it nearly sloshed over the rim. She took a healthy sip.

Why does he make me so nervous?

If she'd met him in her business attire, and this wasn't a semidate, she'd be confident. In control. She frequently negotiated with business executives in her work. She wasn't easily intimidated, regardless of how rich or powerful those men were.

However, in a tiny red dress that left little of her legs and back to the imagination, she felt like a warrior going to battle without a stitch of armor.

Liam drank his wine, silently awaiting her answer.

"Sorry, I don't do this much." She took another sip from her wineglass.

"You don't do what much?" He was definitely enjoying this.

"Date." She immediately regretted her word choice. "Not that this is a date."

"Isn't it?"

"It's a dinner date, but it isn't a date-date. Does that make sense?" *Of course not.* She was babbling like a loon.

The smirk he tried to suppress brimmed over in his dark eyes. He set his glass on the table. "And why is it that a gorgeous woman like you doesn't date much?"

"Because I'm…" *A single mother of two beautiful little girls.* The words caught at the back of her throat, taking her by surprise. It was the most natural thing in the world for her to say. She repeated the words, nearly by rote, every time she met someone new in a nonbusiness setting. Being Sofia and Gabriella's mother was her primary identity, no matter what else she did in her life. She was fine with that, because she adored her daughters. Loved them more than anything in the world. Yet, as she looked at Liam, his eyes dancing over her skin, drinking her in like she was the most fascinating woman he'd ever met, something in the pit of her stomach wouldn't allow the words to escape her mouth.

Would he look at her differently? Would she suddenly seem less attractive?

It was her birthday. The last of her twenties. For one night she could sit through a gourmet meal she didn't have to cook and have an adult conversation with a man who thought she was beautiful. A man whose appreciative gaze made her feel beautiful—something she hadn't felt in a while.

What was the harm in living out the fantasy for one hour of dinner conversation? She wouldn't lie to him. But he was a stranger. He didn't need her full biography. She'd give him the annotated version instead.

Maya cleared her throat. "I work for a small nonprofit organization. The community need is greater than our available resources, so we're seriously understaffed. Keeps me busy. Between that and everything else in my life, there's not much time for dating."

There. Question answered.

"Everything else, like what?"

"I volunteer for a variety of organizations." *Also true. The PTA, the local girls' club and the girls' soccer league.*

The server arrived with their salads before he could pose his next question. Glad for the distraction, Maya returned the conversation to him. "How long have you been in Pleasure Cove?"

His knowing grin indicated her maneuver hadn't gone unnoticed. "A few months."

"And how long will you stay?"

"For the next year, maybe two." He didn't look happy about it.

Maya wanted to ask why, but it felt too personal. She opted for safer topics like the weather and restaurants around town she'd recommend.

"So, how many birthday licks shall I administer this evening?"

So much for safe topics.

"Most women would consider that question rude." She picked up her wineglass. "But I don't mind telling you. I turned twenty-nine today. Too old for birthday licks."

His eyes danced. "Spanking not your style, then?"

Maya nearly choked on her wine. She set the glass down roughly. He was teasing her to see how she'd react. Still, it was better to be clear about where the night was going, or rather where it wasn't. "Let's just file that under Things You'll Never Need to Know." His hearty chuckle made her laugh, too. She shook her head. "The moment I saw you, I knew you were trouble."

He shrugged. "Some might agree. Though it's often a case of being misunderstood, despite my clearly stated intentions. How can I possibly be to blame for such a thing?"

Maya took a piece of French bread from the basket and dipped it into the plate of herb-infused olive oil. She raised her eyes to his. "So the brokenhearted women you've probably left in your wake…they were all to blame?"

His eyes widened with surprise, then narrowed as he watched her eat her bread. "I'm not one for long-drawn-out relationships," he stated without apology. "I don't see how I could possibly be any clearer about it."

Maya laughed. "The thing is, we don't believe you when you say that. We're convinced you just haven't found the right woman. That we'll be the one to make an honest man out of you. So, unless you find a woman who has zero interest in a long-term relationship, you're going to break her heart, whether you intend to or not."

Liam looked thoughtful, almost sad for a moment, as he sipped his wine. He shifted in his seat, back pressed against the chair. "Wish I'd had that bit of wisdom a few years ago. I appreciate your honesty. Isn't there a rule against cluing the dafter sex in on the secrets of dealing with womankind?"

She absently stroked her nearly empty wineglass as she admired his handsome features. "It'll be our little secret."

Chapter 2

Liam studied Maya as she spoke, her lips shiny with olive oil, her hands gesturing wildly. There was something about her he found intriguing. Her smile was adorable, like a mischievous imp who'd pulled a naughty prank and expected to be discovered at any moment. Her laugh was genuine, infectious. It lit her entire face, like the candle inside of the paper lantern on the table between them. Every time she laughed his chest filled with a deep but inexplicable sense of gratification at being the source of it.

The light danced off her glossy tresses gathered in a messy updo. Her hair was a deep chocolate brown, like a decadent torte, streaked with warm caramel highlights. How would her hair look grazing the smooth brown skin of her bare shoulders? How would her soft curves feel pressed against the hard planes of his body? If he played his cards right, he'd find out by the end of the night.

Maya was beautiful, but a direct contrast to the tall, thin blondes to whom he'd gravitated during this five-year binge of serial dating and one-night stands. His interest in them didn't extend beyond his bedroom walls. Theirs didn't extend any further than his family name—and the nine figures in the Westbrook family bank account.

It was a side effect of being the son of a well-known businessman. Women heard his last name and imagined themselves as members of the Westbrook family—with all that it entailed. But that ship sank five years ago, taking any chance of him entertaining thoughts of matrimony along with it. He was satisfied to paint the town with women who looked good on his arm and whose bodies offered a few hours of warmth and comfort. He desired nothing more.

Maya caught his eye because she was stunning. Yet, she was so self-conscious in that sexy little red dress that hugged her body and highlighted her curvy frame. Flirting with her came second nature. He hardly realized he was doing it. However, he had no real designs on her. He was simply being polite.

When he invited her to dine with him, his intentions had been innocent, pure. Two words he'd rarely attribute to himself. Despite rumors that stated otherwise, he did possess a bloody heart. There she was, disappointed and alone on her birthday with some old codger staring down her dress, so he'd asked her to join him for dinner. Partly because he felt sorry for her. Partly because he was afraid she might actually take the dodgy old bastard up on his offer. It was to be his good deed for the day. Perhaps the week.

They'd have dinner. Then he'd walk away. It was the gentlemanly thing to do. But she was feisty and charming. Then there was the way she filled out that dress with those scrumptious curves. Still, he had every intention of being a very good boy—until she insisted she had no intention of sleeping with him.

He never could resist a good challenge.

As he sat opposite her, his resolve to keep their dinner date strictly platonic began to dissolve. He was mesmerized by her luscious lips and the teasing pink tongue that kept darting out to lick them. His body tensed, excited by the sensation of how they'd both feel sliding along his member.

So much for being a very *good boy.*

He adjusted in his seat, nodding as she spoke. Only she wasn't speaking anymore. She stared at him expectantly. "Sorry. You were saying?"

"What do you do at the resort?" She sliced into the land portion of her surf and turf.

He cleared his throat. This was where their casual evening could quickly go off the rails. The Westbrook name obviously meant nothing to her, for which he was grateful. However, revealing that his family owned the resort and dozens of other luxury hotels in ten countries could have much the same result, which would be unfortunate. He was enjoying their easy banter.

"I'm on the management team," he said. "And you? You said you work for an NGO?"

She nodded. "I'm the program coordinator at the Leila Arts Foundation. We're a small organization, so everyone does a little of everything."

"You must enjoy your work. You're practically glowing." He took a bite of his lobster.

"I do. We help underserved members of the community get a fresh start. It's something I can relate to." She looked uneasy. Her gaze dropped to her plate, as if she'd do anything to reel those words back in before she'd spoken them.

He wouldn't press. No point in ruining the mood. They were having such a lovely time. Besides, there was a topic he'd much rather discuss. "No more talk about work. It's your birthday, after all. Let's discuss how we plan to spend the rest of the evening."

"Liam, this—" she indicated the plates on the table between them with her open palm "—is the extent of our evening. I appreciate the dinner invitation, and it's been fun—"

"Then why not continue it? Unless, of course, you doubt you'd be able to resist my charms, since you've declared we won't be sleeping together, and all."

She narrowed her gaze and sat taller. "It would be rude to impose on you any further." Her response was an open invitation for him to overcome her objection.

He grinned inwardly. "I asked you, so you wouldn't be imposing. Consider it a favor."

Her almond-shaped eyes narrowed, and she scrunched her adorable nose. He could practically see the wheels turning in her head. "What do you have in mind?"

"An unforgettable evening."

"Modest, aren't you?" The corner of her mouth curved, almost imperceptibly. "And what is it that will make this night so memorable?"

"You've taken my most surefire weapon off the table." He smirked, watching for her reaction.

Maya averted her eyes. She tried, unsuccessfully, not to smile.

His grin widened. "Fortunately, I have an impressive backup plan. A night of dance."

"You don't strike me as the dancing type." She raised an eyebrow and tucked a few strands of hair behind her ear. Did she know how enticing a move it was?

"I was referring to the ballet. A friend held two seats for me. Have you ever seen *Swan Lake*?"

"Never been to a professional ballet. We don't get much of that here. But I've always wanted to go." Her eyes danced with excitement.

The town's expansion of cultural offerings had been one of the requirements he'd negotiated in the deal to bring their resort to Pleasure Cove. "Then this is your chance. If you don't go, that ticket will go to waste."

Maya twirled a strand of her curly hair around her finger as she carefully assessed him. "I should call it a night."

He kept his countenance neutral. The trick with reeling in catch was not to jerk the line too soon. One of the few worthwhile lessons he'd learned from his older brother, who was otherwise an untrustworthy cretin. Maya wanted to go to the ballet with him. He was sure of it. She just needed a bit of convincing. He could help with that. Liam opened his palm and extended it to her. "Take out your phone."

She stared at him, puzzled. Still, she reached into her purse and produced her phone, clutching it to her chest.

"Excuse me, miss," he called to their server as she walked by. "Would you take a picture of my friend and me?"

A syrupy smile, typically reserved for toothless babies in prams, spread across the woman's face. "Sure."

Liam nodded toward the server, indicating that Maya should give the woman her phone to take the picture.

Maya opened the camera, then handed the phone to her. The woman took their photo and then returned the phone.

He thanked her, then turned to Maya. "Send that picture and a picture of my driver's license—" he placed it on the table in front of her "—to your sister. Let her know you'll be with me this evening. Would that make you feel better?" He watched her expectantly, not saying another word. If he pushed too hard he'd spook her.

Maya furrowed her brows, hesitating for a moment. She sighed, then took a photo of his license, typed out a message on her phone, then hit Send. "Looks like you've got yourself a date."

"So we've graduated to a date-date." He lifted his wineglass and took a sip. Maya laughed. A melodious sound he might never get his fill of. "Tonight will be no mere date. Tonight, we go on an adventure."

"To unforgettable adventures." She raised her glass, clinking it against his.

Liam finished his glass of wine. A victory libation. She'd accepted his challenge, and he'd accepted hers. Because by the end of the evening, he had every intention of having Maya Alvarez in his bed.

Maya's phone rang moments after she sent the message. *Of course.* No way could she send pictures of Hot Suit Guy to Kendra without expecting a call. If she didn't answer the phone, Kendra would keep calling. "I'm sorry, but I need to take this."

Amusement danced beneath his penetrating dark eyes. His gaze was drawn appreciatively to the fabric pulled taut across the sensitive, beaded tips of her breasts. "I'll order dessert."

Her cheeks burned, and she felt a rush of liquid pooling between her thighs. Legs wobbling, she swallowed hard, grabbed her purse and left the table. She could feel his intense stare on her retreating back. Her flesh tingled, as if his gaze seared her skin.

Maya ducked into the restroom, pressed her back against the wall and exhaled. She'd allowed Liam to unnerve her. It was unlike her.

Was he gorgeous? Sure. Rich? Obviously. But she was no consolation prize either. Maybe she wasn't the tiny-waisted siren she'd once been, but she still turned heads, dammit. He should be grateful she'd accepted his offer of companionship for the evening.

Companionship. God, it made him sound like an escort. Or maybe she was the escort. Which was ten times worse.

The phone rang again. She answered in a hushed tone. "Yes."

"Are you serious right now?" Kendra's voice was also muted. From the muffled sound of a PA announcement in the background, Kendra was still at the hospital.

"Am I that pathetic?" She was only half teasing.

"No, honey. Of course not. I'm just saying, dude looks like a freakin' model. Where'd you meet him?"

"Here at the restaurant. He knew I was alone on my birthday, so he invited me to have dinner with him."

"I can't believe you accepted his invitation. There's hope for you yet."

"Don't get so excited. It's not like I'm gonna sleep with the guy. I told him that."

"You said those actual words to him? Yet, he's still taking you to the ballet? Okay, now I really like this guy." The background of Kendra's call was silent, like she'd gone somewhere quieter. "Maya, I'm thrilled you're getting out there again. A night out on the town with a handsome guy is just what the doctor ordered."

"It does feel nice to relax for one night and just be... me. Not mommy, you know? God, that sounds selfish." She was suddenly conscious of whether the other women in the restroom were listening. Judging her.

"No, it doesn't. You're an amazing mother. You deserve to have some fun. Tonight is about you. Have a blast. Call me in the morning by ten, so I know you're okay. I'll take you to a belated birthday lunch tomorrow."

"Sounds good. I'll call you when I get home. Tonight."

Maya ended the call and inhaled deeply, hardly able to believe she was going out with a man she'd just met. She'd been struggling lately with a stifling feeling of suffocation. Her life was the same song playing endlessly on repeat. She'd been trying her best to suppress a growing desire to do something different. Unexpected. A bit naughty even. Maybe ignoring the feeling wasn't the answer. Maybe what she needed was to get it out of her system once and for all. With Liam.

No. No, that's ridiculous. Insane. I can't.

She took out her lip gloss—a pale, barely there pink—and reapplied. She'd insisted there would be no sex, and that was best. So why was there a flutter low in her belly at the mere possibility of it?

Visions of Maya Alvarez naked in his bed flooded Liam's brain. He wanted her. Needed those heart-stopping curves beneath him as he reached his pinnacle. To hear her call his name in that adorable accent she reverted to occasionally. And he wanted her to want him, too. To plead for it.

His eyes traveled the length of her body as she approached the table. He outlined her shapely figure, staking his claim and mapping the trail his tongue would take along her skin. "I was beginning to think you'd slipped out the back door."

"Why? Does that happen to you a lot?"

He laughed. "Define *a lot*."

"Oh God." She swept a loose curl behind her ear, lines crinkling around her dark eyes. "What on earth have I gotten myself into?"

Chapter 3

Swan Lake was divine. Maya sat beside Liam, barely able to hold back the emotions evoked by the tragic, beautiful finale.

She sniffled and wiped the corner of her eye with the back of her finger, refusing to glance in his direction. They barely knew each other. No way she'd let him see her cry.

They were both on their feet applauding during the curtain call. Liam reached inside his jacket and handed her a handkerchief.

She accepted the offering. "I'm not crying."

"Right. Figured it was allergies."

The lights rose in the house and patrons made their way toward the exits. Liam placed a hand low on her back and guided her toward the stage, against the crush of the opening-night crowd.

"Isn't the exit in the other direction?" She glanced back at him.

There was that damned smirk again. It was enticing, and so was he.

"It is. But, I have a surprise for you. How'd you like to meet Karina Alexandrova, the dancer who plays the Swan Queen?"

Maya halted, turning to face him. "You…you know her?"

"Friend of a friend and all that."

"And it won't be any trouble? She must be exhausted after her performance."

"It'll be fine. Promise."

Butterflies fluttered in her stomach. She'd seen her first ballet that didn't involve her daughters. *Swan Lake*, no less. Now, she was going to meet the principal ballerina of a highly acclaimed company. A rarity in Pleasure Cove. Liam had delivered on his promise of a memorable evening. But beside the elation at the prospect of meeting Karina, a growing sense of sadness lodged in her chest.

Her night with Liam was coming to an end.

They were escorted to Karina's dressing room. She answered the door in the silk robe he'd given her after his trip to Japan two years ago. Her damp corn-silk blond hair hung in loose waves on her thin shoulders.

"Liam, how lovely to see you." She leaned in and let him kiss her cheek before turning to Maya. "And who is this gorgeous creature?" The smile plastered on her face was nearly convincing.

Maya's eyes widened like she was surprised the great Karina Alexandrova had deigned to acknowledge her. There was something about Maya that was refreshingly unpretentious. It was endearing.

She extended her hand. "Maya. Alvarez. It's a pleasure to meet you, Ms. Alexandrova. Your performance tonight was brilliant."

Karina's tight smile relaxed into a more genuine one.

No quicker way to the woman's heart than to recognize her outstanding balletic skills. Even nearing the end of her career, no one could pull off double and triple fouettés with the skill, beauty and sheer will of Karina Alexandrova. "Thank you, Maya. And please, call me Karina. All my friends do. And any friend of Liam's is certainly a friend of mine." She shifted her gaze to him.

Liam nodded toward the roses on her dressing table. "I see you got the flowers."

"Yes, and they are very beautiful. Thank you. You always know how to make a girl feel special." Karina gave him a knowing grin, then turned back to his date. "Maya, have you ever been backstage at a performance?" Maya shook her head. "Then we must make this a special occasion. Several members of the company are having a small opening-night reception, if you'd like to meet some of the other dancers. Would you like that?"

Maya's eyes danced. *Utterly adorable.* "I would."

Karina opened the door and summoned a stagehand. She poked her head back inside the dressing room. "Gordo will walk you over to the reception. If you don't mind, I need to borrow Liam for a moment or two. Then I'll send him right over."

Maya glanced at him, her brows furrowed. He nodded, his arms crossed as he leaned against a dressing table. "I'll catch up with you shortly," he said. A message meant for both Maya and Karina.

She smiled in response, then thanked Karina before following Gordo down the hall.

Karina locked the door, then stood with her back pressed against it. She pursed her lips and gave him that look. The one that always meant trouble.

"I wasn't sure you'd come." She inched closer, her gaze gliding down the length of his body.

"Neither was I. After all, the last time we saw each

other you chucked a metal garbage can at my head. Only missed it by this much." He held up his thumb and forefinger to demonstrate. "Forgive me if I was a little skeptical when you offered opening-night tickets for me and a guest. How'd you know I was here in Pleasure Cove? Last time we spoke I was still in LA."

"A girl has her ways. And as for our little…misunderstanding, you know us ballerinas. We're a temperamental lot." She shrugged, a feigned look of innocence on her face. "I said I was sorry, didn't I?"

Liam chuckled. "You did indeed. Thank you for the tickets. I was debating whether to use them when I discovered Maya had never been to the ballet. Seemed like fate."

Karina stepped as close as his long legs, stretched out in front of him, would allow. Frustrated by the barrier he'd created between them, she folded her arms and pursed her lips. "I know I left you a guest ticket, but I hoped you'd come alone."

"Still reigning queen of the mixed signal, I see."

"I would think you'd understand them by now." She pouted.

He did. In fact, before meeting Maya, he'd been debating whether to take Karina up on her offer. Doing so would've been a mistake. He realized that now. "Karina, you're a talented, beautiful woman, and I adore you. But we've been down this road before, love. Time to stop bashing our heads against the wall."

She turned her back to him and strode toward her dressing table on the other side of the room. Raising her eyes, she met the reflection of his gaze in the mirror.

"I was angry before, and I apologize for that. We agreed to an open relationship. Then I changed the rules. It was wrong of me. I realize that now."

"Appreciate the apology." His posture softened. "Doesn't change the fact that you want more than I can give you.

You deserve to be happy. I want that for you, but it's not something I'm prepared to offer. Sorry, love."

She crossed the room and stood in front of him again. "I don't need anything more. I can be happy with things the way they were."

"No, you can't." Liam stood. He gripped Karina's shoulders and kissed her forehead. "And we both know it."

He walked to the door and unlocked it.

"What about Maya?" Karina's voice was shaky. "Can you give her what she deserves?"

He slipped out of her dressing room without a response. It was a question best left unanswered.

Chapter 4

By the time he found Maya, she'd drunk two glasses of champagne and met nearly half the ballet company. They stepped outside the theater and into the warm night air. The salty breeze coming off the Atlantic Ocean rustled loose strands of her hair. Her skin glistened in the light of the moon shining brightly above. She'd been practically giddy back at the party. Suddenly, she seemed sad.

"What's wrong?"

Maya shook her head. The knot she wore at the back of her head had loosened and hung low over her right shoulder. "Nothing. Tonight was incredible. Just like you promised. Thank you. I had a wonderful time."

"What, you think the night is over? It's not even midnight."

"Way past my bedtime." She laughed.

"That saddens me deeply." He chuckled. "Besides, it's your birthday. That warrants an exception, wouldn't you say? You'd planned to go to a jazz club with your sister tonight. So let's do it."

"You listen to jazz? Really?" Arms crossed, she regarded him as if he were trying to convince her that the earth was flat.

"Don't look so surprised. I'm a man of many interests. Classic American jazz happens to be one of them."

"Who's your favorite jazz artist?"

"Miles Davis, though I'm also partial to John Coltrane and Dave Brubeck."

"Favorite Miles album?" She narrowed her gaze.

He smiled. "Is that even a question? *Kind of Blue*, of course."

Shoulders relaxed, she nodded her agreement. "There's a small jazz club near the waterfront that plays live music on Friday nights. The place is a dive, but the music is excellent and the martinis are fantastic. We missed the earlier jazz band, but they play Latin jazz at midnight. There'll be dancing, if you like that sort of thing."

"Spent a few holidays knocking about South America. My samba is a little rusty, but I do an impressive mambo." He winked.

"Is that right?" She smiled, eyes twinkling. "Well, that's something I seriously need to see."

At the jazz club, the ten-piece band crowded the small stage. The vocalist belted out a song over the blare of the horns and the rhythm of the bongos and congas. The dense Friday night crowd, comprised mostly of tourists, pressed in all around them. However, Liam's focus was on only one thing: Maya.

She was stunning in that strapless red dress. Released from the knot, her loose curls grazed her bare shoulders as she swayed her hips to the music in ways that made portions of his anatomy sit up and take notice. She was relaxed. Openly flirtatious.

The alcohol she'd consumed no doubt contributed to her

relaxed state of mind. Yet, she wasn't drunk. She was less guarded. More comfortable in her own skin.

On the dance floor, she owned her beauty. Embraced her sensuality. When they first met, she almost seemed embarrassed by it.

The band took a break and the female vocalist started singing a slow romantic ballad accompanied only by the guitarist and keyboardist.

Maya turned to leave the dance floor, but Liam caught her hand in his. Turning back to him, she smiled. One arm slung low across her back, he pulled her against him. He gripped her hand, intoxicated by her soft, floral scent and the delicious sensation of her body nestled against his as they swayed to the beat.

Her initial tension gave way. She relaxed, leaning in to him. "So what got you interested in jazz?"

"My best mate, Wesley. He's an American expat. We met in boarding school at thirteen and eventually became roommates. His dad was a jazz musician. Took off when he was around ten. Sometimes Wes would play the old classics. Music his dad listened to when he was growing up. His way of holding on to the good memories, I guess."

"I listened to jazz with my dad every Saturday morning while he tinkered in his workshop in the garage. Miles Davis, Charlie Parker, Thelonious Monk, Ella Fitzgerald, Etta James. Seems like one of them was the soundtrack to every important conversation I've ever had with my dad." A wistful smile lit her brown eyes.

"Does your sister like jazz, too?"

"No." The warm smile in her eyes was gone. "Kendra hates jazz for the same reason I love it. It reminds her of our father. She tolerates it on special occasions like my birthday."

"Then she is a very good sister, indeed."

"She is. I couldn't ask for a better one."

He pulled her closer and they continued to dance in

companionable silence. The night had turned out different than he expected. Then again, so had she. Maya was opinionated, yet charming. Astute, yet amusing. She possessed a curious sensuality she seemed terrified to acknowledge, let alone explore. There was nothing he wanted more than to help her do just that. His desire for her coursed through his veins like adrenaline.

She broke the silence between them. "I have to admit, you are a pretty good dancer."

"Pretty good?" He scoffed. "You haven't seen the half of what I can do."

Liam twirled Maya, pulled her in close, then dipped her, his face inches from hers as he held her in his arms. Her eyes widened in surprise. His gaze dropped to the little O her mouth formed as her breath came in short bursts. He returned his gaze to hers and slowly brought her vertical again, neither of them moving.

His heart pounded. There was something in her eyes. Something he couldn't explain. Liam pulled her closer and pressed his lips to hers. Maya went completely still, then slowly relaxed, slipping her arms around his waist, beneath his suit jacket.

She tasted sweet and rich like a decadent dessert you couldn't get enough of but knew you would regret in the morning. His mind raced, wanting to taste her skin. To be enveloped in her scent.

Her kiss, raw and hungry, evoked a reaction from his body. He wanted her. But not here, not like this.

He tore his mouth from hers, despite his body's insistence for more.

Maya shuffled backward, fingers pressed to her parted lips.

The kiss had taken them both by surprise. He wasn't in the habit of snogging in the middle of a crowded dance floor. He should apologize for being so forward. Still, he wasn't sorry he'd done it. "I don't know what came over me." *That much is true.* "But—"

Before he could finish his sentence, one man swung at another man who stood directly behind Maya. Only the man was ducking out of the way.

Liam pulled Maya to him. The man's fist just missed the back of her head. He shoved her behind him, his vision blurred with rage.

"Hey, asshole!" He snatched the man by his collar. "You nearly struck my date."

The man smelled as if he'd bathed with a bottle of gin. He swung at him, but Liam blocked his punch and shoved the man backward. The second man took the opportunity to land a sucker punch that connected with the first man's jaw. A third man—a friend of the first—landed a punch that connected with Liam's cheekbone. A throbbing pain exploded behind his left eye.

It'd been a long time since he'd taken a hit like that.

He drew his fist back to hit the man, but froze when Maya shrieked his name. He wasn't alone and things were going sideways fast.

Liam grabbed Maya's hand. "I'm going to get you out of here. Stay close to me, all right?"

They made their way through the crush of bodies. Some headed toward the exit. Others pressed toward the growing fight.

The house lights came on and the club owner announced that the police were on their way. Bouncers made their way toward the ruckus and tried to pull apart the drunken brawlers.

By the time Liam and Maya made their way outside, police cars had arrived and were blocking the exit of the lot where his car was parked. They kept walking until they were in front of a little gift shop around the corner. Head throbbing, Liam pressed his back against the brick wall.

He winced as he forced a grin. "Hadn't planned quite this much excitement."

Maya placed a gentle hand on his jaw and tried to get a good look at his cheek under the streetlight. "We need to get some ice on that. Wait here. I'll get some from the bartender."

"You can't go back in there." His voice reverberated in his brain. "Who knows how insane things have gotten? Besides, technically, I was involved in the brawl that got this whole melee started."

The headlines back home would scream "Westbrook family heir arrested in beachside barroom brawl. *Again.*" Way to show his father he was focused and serious about succeeding him as CEO of the company.

"We need to get ice from somewhere or this side of your face is going to be three times the size of that one."

Liam nodded down the street. "I live in that building. It's a couple of blocks from here."

Maya surveyed the glass-and-steel structure. Head tilted, she shifted her gaze to him. As if trying to decide whether this was part of some dodgy plan to bed her.

It was.

Though he'd planned a smoother transition that didn't include some bloke's fist connecting with his cheekbone. One of his best features, if he was to believe the magazines back home.

Liam grimaced as he reached into his pocket. "The address is on my li—"

Maya held her hand up. "Just c'mon before the buzz wears off and I change my mind." She pursed her pink lips. "By the way…thank you. That's twice in one night you've rescued me."

"Self-preservation, love. I wasn't saving you. I was afraid that guy was going to knock you into me." Liam tried to suppress a smile, but his cheeks rose. He winced.

Maya laughed. "Well, whatever the case, it's time I return the favor."

He stood, his head throbbing. He draped an arm around her shoulders as they made their way the two blocks to his flat.

Chapter 5

An uneasiness grew in Maya's chest as they approached the twelve-story structure. It wasn't fear. She felt comfortable with Liam.

Too comfortable.

They barely knew each other. Yet, something in his penetrating stare made her feel as if he knew her intimately, in ways she didn't quite know herself.

He instinctively seemed to know what she wanted. The most unnerving part? So far he'd been right.

Until the brawl at the club cut their night short, they'd been having a fabulous evening. Magical even. Maya cringed. That last martini must've gone straight to her head. She was a grown-ass woman who knew from experience there was nothing magical about love and relationships. Not that this was either.

Still, she couldn't shake the heightened sensation that vibrated through her body, making it harder to breathe as her mind returned to the kiss they'd shared. The roughness of his beard. The way he held her in his arms. Nor could she escape the unrelenting desire to experience it again.

Everything about her night with Liam was a dreamy indulgence that might never come again.

"You're quiet." His voice, low and warm, seemed to apologize for intruding on her thoughts. "Haven't changed your mind, have you?"

"And abandon you midrescue? No way." She stopped and pulled out her phone. "This is a beautiful building. Mind if I take a picture of it?"

He smiled knowingly. "Of course not. Only when you tell your sister about the brawl, make me look good, will you?"

Maya laughed as she snapped a photo of the building, which included its name, The Jameson, highlighted in tall neon letters. She dashed off a quick text to Kendra with a brief note: Hanging out at Liam's place. Don't get the wrong idea. Long story.

They entered the large, bright lobby of the newly renovated industrial building and took the elevator to the penthouse level. Glass windows in the corridor rose another full story.

"I thought the penthouse was always on the top floor." She surveyed the space, mesmerized by the view of the water.

"These units occupy the two top floors." He opened the door and stepped inside, holding his hand out to her. "I'll show you."

Last chance to change your mind.

Fighting the jittery sensation that turned her stomach inside out, she inhaled deeply, put her hand in his and stepped inside.

The dim lighting enhanced the view of the skyline along the waterfront. The windows spanned the entire length of one wall, affording a view of the Atlantic Ocean.

"What an amazing view." She slipped her heels off and left them by the entrance. An instant relief after a night of dancing and the walk to Liam's place.

"I don't need to put raw steak on my face, do I?" His voice echoed across the hardwood floors from where he stood in the kitchen.

Maya padded toward the kitchen and stood beside him. She plucked a bag of frozen peas out of the open freezer drawer, then positioned them on his swollen cheek. "You must have a hell of a headache. You should sit down."

He shifted his jaw from side to side and winced. "Nothing a stiff drink can't rectify. Can I get you anything?"

"I drank more tonight than I have in the past six months. Just water, please."

Liam stepped behind his well-stocked bar and handed her a bottle of sparkling mineral water from the mini fridge. He filled his glass with an amber-colored liquor. "I admire your restraint. I don't share it, but I do admire it. Should you change your mind and decide to join me, let me know."

"I'm impressed." Maya sank onto the sofa.

"Why?" He sat beside her.

"You didn't put the peas down once. You're pretty proficient with one hand."

"I am indeed." Waggling his brows, he flashed a smile that warmed her nearly as much as the kiss had.

Heat spread through her cheeks. "About that headache…" She stood, putting space between them. "Can I get you something for it?"

"Yes, please." He repositioned the bag. "In the cabinet over the kitchen sink."

Maya grabbed the pills from the cabinet and a bottle of water from the fridge. She handed both items to him, then knelt on the couch beside him. Lifting the bag of frozen peas, she inspected his face.

"What's the verdict, doc?"

"The swelling is subsiding, but now bruises are forming on your cheek and underneath your eye."

"Bugger. No chance that'll resolve itself by eight a.m. on Monday. Better concoct a tall tale. I was attacked by two hooligans while defending an intriguing young woman whose extraordinary beauty had me completely mesmerized." He grazed her cheekbone with his thumb, his fingers resting gently on her neck.

Maya shuddered inwardly. His gaze was filled with a white-hot heat as tantalizing as a flame to an unsuspecting moth. She could see it as clearly as the sun in a cloudless sky. Yet, she couldn't turn away.

Her skin flamed beneath his touch. Heat crawled down her neck and into the beaded tips of her breasts, culminating at the simmering junction between her thighs. Liam glided his thumb across her lower lip. Her heart skipped a beat, her breathing shallow. The hungry look in his dark eyes went straight to her head, making her dizzy with desire.

Liam tightened his grip on her neck, pulling her closer until his lips met hers. Maya's lids drifted closed as he placed soft kisses on one side of her mouth then the other. Her skin vibrated with alternate sensations. The contrast of his beard grazing her skin with the delicate caress of his lips like butterfly wings whispering against her skin. Gentle and sweet, yet surprisingly erotic.

She was playing a dangerous game.

Her brain understood this. Every other part of her anatomy disagreed.

Maya dropped the frozen peas and tangled her chilly fingers in his dark curls. Her other hand braced his shoulder, enjoying the delicious feeling of the hard, taut muscles there.

Liam slid one hand to her waist, his fingers pressing into

her spine, pulling her closer as he deepened the kiss. He sucked her lower lip between his, then glided his tongue along the ridge between her lips. God help her, she made a noise reminiscent of a purr as she parted her lips, granting him access.

He glided his tongue against hers, then gently grazed her palate. Liam's mouth tasted of the liquor he'd just consumed. A smoky, rich flavor. Chocolate with the slightest hint of berries. He let out a low hum that vibrated in her throat as his hand glided down her side, and then down her leg. Wrapping his fingers around her thigh, he pulled her onto his lap so she straddled him.

The pressure of his steely length pressed against her swollen folds sent a shock of bliss throughout her body—already wound as taut as a violin string. She gasped, breaking their kiss, as she tried to catch her breath and coax her traitorous body back to reality.

Hooking up with random guys was for pretty young coeds, not for single moms. She was sensible, reliable. The woman who shuttled her daughters to their soccer games, made brownies for the bake sale and sewed sunflower costumes for the school play. She wasn't this person: rash and bold. Passionate and daring.

Not anymore.

She'd buried that girl years ago. Right around the time her first daughter was born. No matter how handsome and charming Liam Westbrook was, and despite the fact that he'd mastered the art of the orgasmic French kiss, it was time to say goodbye.

He planted soft, wet kisses on her jaw and down her throat that rendered her speechless. She wrapped her arms around his neck and let out a quiet moan. He gripped her bottom and squeezed the flesh there.

It hurt.

Yet the pain sent a corresponding jolt of pleasure

straight to her aching core. She ground her pelvis against his, desperate to intensify the feeling building at her center.

Liam pressed a hand to her back. The other slid along her thigh and underneath her dress, cupping her sex through her silky underwear, damp with her arousal. She shuddered and sighed.

You're playing with fire, girl. You know what happens when you play with fire...you get burned.

The little voice in the back of her head was the equivalent of an icy shower.

She clutched his wrist and dragged it from underneath her dress.

Liam's handsome face was etched with concern. "Have I upset you?"

She shook her head, lowering her eyes as she climbed off him and scrambled to her feet.

"No, it isn't you. It's me. I...I can't do this, I'm sorry." Maya paced the floor. "I wasn't thinking. I shouldn't have allowed things to get this far."

Liam sprang to his feet. He winced, the agonizing pain evident in his eyes. He gathered himself, placing gentle hands on her shoulders. His forced smile nearly masked his disappointment. "No apology necessary. Really."

He stepped out onto the terrace. After peering over the railing, he returned, his face pinched with a frown.

"The police are still there." He picked up the peas and put the bag to his cheek. "We still can't reach my car."

Maya scraped her teeth over her lower lip. The muscles in her abdomen tightened.

Liam held one hand up, palm facing her. "Not to worry. We'll grab a cab, and I'll escort you back to your car."

She walked toward him, her hand out, fingers wriggling until he handed over the bag of peas. "These aren't cold anymore." She didn't acknowledge his offer. Instead, she went to the kitchen, tossed the bag inside the freezer and retrieved a bag of brussels sprouts. Maya stepped close enough to position the bag on his face. He watched her without comment.

"Your head is pounding. I can see it in your eyes." She nodded toward the couch. "Stay here and lie down. I can take a cab back on my own."

"Unescorted? At this time of the morning?" He lowered the bag and stared at her in disbelief. "Surely you're joking. I would never forgive myself if something were to happen to you."

"I'm a big girl." She stepped toward him. "I'll be fine."

"If you don't want me in the cab with you, that's fine. I'll follow in another to make sure you get off safely."

"You need to sit and rest." She guided his hand so that the frozen vegetables were on his cheek again. "And keep this on your face if you want the rest of that swelling to go down."

"Either we both go or... Never mind."

"Or *what*?" She was almost afraid to ask, but something inside her wanted to know.

"You're welcome to spend the night in my guest suite." He raised his free hand in response to the objection forming on her face. "The door locks internally, and there isn't a key from the outside. You'll be completely safe, I assure you."

Maya studied his dark eyes. The usual levity gone, his offer felt sincere. "I'll stay under one condition. You need to understand this doesn't change anything between us."

"Duly noted." The look of mild amusement returned to his handsome face. "I'll show you to your room whenever you're ready."

Chapter 6

Maya's eyes fluttered open. Her cell phone blared, each note a rubber mallet hammering her skull.

Heavy drapes filtered the light coming in through the large windows of what clearly wasn't her tiny, dark apartment bedroom. She lay tangled in a soft blanket, cashmere maybe. Her dress lay neatly across a chair in the corner, and she was wearing an oversize T-shirt.

Maya rolled toward the sound of Kendra's ringtone. Her cell phone—perched on the nightstand—stopped ringing, giving her pounding head a reprieve. She'd had a lot to drink. No wonder she felt like hell. Probably looked it, too.

Shrugging off the cover, Maya pressed a palm to her forehead and grunted. Kendra called again. She pulled herself upright and reached for the phone.

"Yeah?" was all she could manage.

"Maya, I've been calling you all morning." Kendra was in full panic mode.

"Sorry. Lost track of time," she mumbled, pulling the

phone away from her ear. Asking Kendra to tone it down would have the same effect as poking a bear in the eye. "What time is it?"

"After noon. You were supposed to call two hours ago. I was one more unanswered call away from sending the cops to see your friend, Liam. That's where you are, I assume."

"Yes." *I think so.* Maya opened her eyes again and glanced around the room. "It's not what you're thinking. I didn't sleep with him."

"I'm not angry because you spent the night." Kendra drew in a deep breath. "I'm upset because you promised to call so I'd know you were okay, but then you didn't. It's not like you. I was worried."

"I overslept, that's all. I promise you, everything is fine. All right?"

Kendra huffed in relief. "As long as you're…wait, what do you mean you didn't sleep with him? You're just camping out at his house having a slumber party?"

"Something like that." Maya glanced toward the door. Footsteps approached. "Look, I gotta go. I'll call you when I get home, okay?"

"And exactly when will that be?" Kendra prodded.

There was a knock at the door. "Hold on a sec," Maya whispered into the phone, and then pressed it to her chest. "Yes?"

"Is it okay if I come in?" Liam's voice sounded huskier than it had the night before.

Maya ran a hand through her hair and wiped her face. Hopefully, she didn't look half as bad as she felt. She opened the door and let him in.

He stepped inside, hovering inside the doorway. The ice had worked. His cheek looked better. The fitted T-shirt and slim navy khakis he wore accentuated his athletic build. "Wanted to check on you. Did you sleep okay?"

"Yes, thank you. Can't believe I slept so late."

"You probably don't usually have a night like last night either."

"A night like what?" Maya could hear Kendra's muffled voice coming from the phone.

"Oh geez." She held up a finger. Liam nodded. "Kendra, I'll call when I'm back home."

"What did he mean by—"

Maya ended the call and tossed the phone onto the bed. "That was my sister. I was supposed to call this morning."

"She must've been worried."

"She was, but everything is fine now. Sorry I slept so long. I'll be out of here in a few minutes. Mind if I use your restroom?"

"Of course not. I left fresh towels for you. In the meantime, I'll make some espresso. That always makes me feel better after a late night out." He turned to leave, calling over his shoulder, "Let me know if you need anything else."

Maya cleared her throat. "You wouldn't have an extra toothbrush, would you?"

He grinned. "Already on the counter. See you in a bit."

"Thanks for understanding about last night, and for not taking advantage of the situation. I don't do my best thinking after a night of drinking." She cringed at the rhyme, hoping he didn't think she was trying to be funny.

He nodded and closed the door behind him.

What did she think he was, an ill-bred barbarian? He wanted her, certainly. But he'd never take advantage of any woman. He was pretty straightforward about what he wanted.

Well, not always.

He hadn't been forthcoming regarding his real objective in bringing her back to his place last night, but she was no naive teenager. He hadn't minced words where his desire for her was concerned. After that kiss they shared on the dance floor, it was clear she wanted him, too.

Liam grabbed the coffee filter and ground his favorite organic espresso roast. He locked the filter into place and watched as the thick, fragrant espresso streamed into two shot glasses. The kiss they shared on his sofa replayed in his mind nearly as vividly as when it happened.

"Smells fantastic." Her voice startled him out of his daze.

"Wait until you have a sip." He turned to face her. Stripped down to a hint of lip gloss, her face was still luminous and her skin was practically flawless. "What can I get you? Espresso? Latte? Mocha latte?"

"You can do that?" She glanced around the kitchen, with its expensive, professional-grade appliances. The only items he used were the espresso machine and the microwave.

"I can, and you're going to love it."

"A mocha latte, then, please." She placed her clutch on the counter and climbed onto the stool.

"Coming right up." He grabbed the milk from the fridge and poured it into the frothing pitcher.

"Thank you for the toothbrush. Lucky thing you had an extra one, huh?" Her teasing tone countered her statement.

"Indeed." He pursed his lips, trying not to smile. So maybe he did purchase toothbrushes and condoms in bulk. One never knew when an opportunity for an unexpected frolic might arise. Better to be prepared, and he was. Always.

Breakfast fare, on the other hand, he kept in short supply. Make an overnight visitor breakfast, and you might as well offer her an invitation to move in. Sharing a morning meal at his place after a night in the sack with a virtual stranger was against his unwritten policy. Instead, he supplied a strong cup of coffee. One that made her sober enough to want to head home. Of course, if a woman was at his apartment the next morning, she'd usually shared his bed the night before. So he found himself in unfamiliar territory.

He needed a reason for her to stay.

"I kept it. The toothbrush." She patted her purse. "It was better than the one I have at home, and it's not like you're going to give it to someone else."

"Well, if you approve of my taste in dental sundries, you're going to love my selection of caffeinated beverages." He whisked in the chocolate powder, added the milk and finally, the froth. Then he created a swirly leaf pattern before setting the cup on a saucer in front of her. "Try this."

She picked up the steaming cup and blew across the top of it. He couldn't tear his eyes away from the little O her mouth formed. She made the most innocent gestures erotic. His body tensed.

"Mmm…" She pulled the cup from her lips, her eyes closed. He shuddered a little. "This is good. I'm impressed."

Oh, I haven't even begun to impress you.

"Excellent." He turned back to the machine and made a café Americano for himself.

They sat at the breakfast bar drinking their coffee. Liam cleared his throat and shifted on the bar stool. "What do you think of breakfast?"

"Is that an invitation, or are you asking my opinion on the benefits of breakfast in general?" She took another sip of her mocha latte.

He laughed. "You're not going to make this easy for me, are you?"

"No," she said. "I don't think I am."

"It's an invitation," he said. "I was just about to order breakfast. Brunch, actually. You're welcome to… I mean, I'd like it very much if you'd stay."

She bit her lip, her heart beating faster as she searched his eyes. They enjoyed each other's company last night. After she turned him down, he'd shown her his jazz collection. He was a purist who collected the classics on vinyl like her dad. She'd thumbed through the album covers that were so familiar to her. Miles Davis. Charlie Parker. Dave Brubeck. John Coltrane. Ella Fitzgerald. They listened to some of their favorites on his high-tech wireless record player while sharing fruit, cheese and an unbelievably good bottle of wine. Even then, she'd been reluctant to finally say good-night. Still, maybe it was better for both of them if she didn't stay.

"C'mon. You won't regret it." The man was charming and slightly irresistible. Besides, what did she have to do that was more important? Without the girls, her weekend plans consisted of doing laundry, some neglected dusting and cooking a meal for one.

She took another sip of her mocha latte and raised her eyes to his.

"Brunch would be nice."

Chapter 7

Liam ordered a selection of brunch items from the restaurant downstairs. Fluffy, delicious waffles served with a side of mixed berries and whipped cream, scrambled eggs, crispy bacon, and freshly squeezed orange and grapefruit juice.

It was a beautiful morning, so he suggested they eat on the upstairs terrace. He was right. The daytime view of the Atlantic Ocean was stunning. She'd moved to Pleasure Cove following her divorce, to be near her half sister and as far away from her ex as possible. Even if that meant moving away from her parents and grandmother. Rarely had she taken a moment like this to truly appreciate the view as the gentle breeze tickled her skin.

"If I had a view like this, I'd eat out here every day. Breakfast, lunch and dinner. Even in winter." She sipped her grapefruit juice as the waves rolled onto the shore.

"You'd change your tune once you had icicles hanging from that adorable nose of yours." His eyes crinkled.

"Besides, it's like anything else. No matter how shiny and amazing it is at first, after a while, the newness wears off."

"Is that why you prefer no-strings-attached relationships? Because you get bored?" She could feel the heat of his stare as she surveyed the horizon.

He cleared his throat. "Don't like complications. Had enough of those in my life."

"Fair enough." She returned her gaze to his and smiled. "Thank you for brunch, Liam. It was wonderful. I hate to eat and run—"

"Then don't. Stay." His dark eyes were insistent.

Maya's stomach was tied in knots. She wanted to stay and live out the vivid fantasies that had been dancing in her head since their kiss, but no good could come of it.

So why is it so hard to say no?

She set down her glass and stood, her eyes not meeting his. "I can't."

"I don't believe you."

She picked up her coffee mug and headed back inside. "Well, it's true."

Liam followed her down the stairs and into the kitchen. Normally, he was much more direct, but Maya had been so reluctant that he hadn't taken that approach with her. Now she was prepared to walk out the door. This was his final shot.

Time to turn up the heat.

He wrapped one arm around her waist and kissed her ear. "Stay."

"This was a mistake. I'm not who you think I am." Her breath hitched as he swept her hair aside and pressed his lips to the base of her neck. She smelled of soap, her skin freshly scrubbed. The floral scent, which had intoxicated him all night, was gone, yet it lingered in his senses.

"You're not Maya Alvarez?"

"Of course I am." Her voice trembled as he planted soft kisses at the spot where her neck and shoulder met.

"The incredibly sexy NGO coordinator with an amazing smile and wicked sense of humor?"

She paused a beat before responding, her chest heaving as her breath came in quick bursts. "Yes."

Liam pulled her closer. Maya didn't object or pull away. She inhaled deeply, then released a small sigh as her bottom nestled against the growing ridge beneath his slacks.

He hadn't misread her cues. Maya wanted to stay. She only needed a little encouragement.

His hand drifted up her body, across her trembling belly, to the swell of her full breasts. He pressed his lips to her ear and lowered the timbre of his voice.

"Then I know *exactly* who you are, and unless I'm gravely mistaken, *this* is precisely what you want. What I can't understand is why you're so determined to fight it."

She turned to face him, her breath ragged as she lightly pressed her fingertips to his biceps. "I'm not this girl. I don't do things like this. I'm a m—"

He pulled her into his arms and kissed her, cutting off her protests. Gripping the back of her neck, he kissed her hard. She melted into him as she kissed him back, fisting handfuls of his shirt.

Liam broke their kiss and placed his hands on either side of her face. His eyes locked with hers. "I want you, Maya. You want me, too, or you wouldn't be standing here with me now. But I need to hear the words. Tell me what you want."

She stared at him in silence, her body trembling as she caught her breath. Her mouth opened without sound. Finally, she whispered, "I want this, to be with you."

He wanted to shag her right there in the kitchen. Hitch that hot little number up over her hips, rip off the silky knickers he'd had the briefest encounter with the night before and bend her over the sink. A shiver ran down his spine at the thought of taking her from behind, buried to the hilt in that sweet little slit.

Yet, she was as skittish as a rabbit. Frightened by her own desires. He needed to take things slow or she'd be scared off, just as she'd been the night before.

Work your way up to the rougher stuff, mate. Start off with a little finesse.

He held his hand out. She regarded it warily before placing her trembling hand in his.

Liam led her to his bedroom. He kissed her slowly, sweetly, before easing her onto his bed. Her eyes were wild with excitement, maybe even a hint of fear. He needed to take his time with her. Put her at ease.

He pressed his mouth to hers. Started with soft, feathery kisses that became deeper. More passionate. She wrapped her leg around him, pulling him in deeper. Her body begged for more, even if she wasn't prepared to give voice to her desires.

Liam glided a hand up her thigh, then underneath her dress. He skimmed his hand across her soft belly. Maya tensed. Perhaps she was self-conscious. She shouldn't have been. He liked the feel of it. Of her. Her body was warm and inviting. He slid his fingers beneath the waistband of her knickers into the patch of soft curls.

A sharp intake of breath signaled that he'd hit her nub, slick and stiff. She was so wet. His knob twitched in anticipation. He'd felt a twinge of guilt earlier. This was what he envisioned from the moment she declared that she wasn't going to sleep with him. As he glided two fingers back and forth over her sex there was no doubt she was as eager as he. He hadn't tricked or deceived her. If anything, he'd freed her to do exactly what she'd desired all along.

Maya dug her nails into his shoulder. Her murmurs grew louder as she rocked her hips against his hand. His knob hardened painfully in response. He pressed his mouth to her ear.

"Glad you stayed, love. Would've been a shame to deprive us of such pleasure."

She inhaled deeply without reply, working her hips against his hand.

His growl deepened. "Tell me you're glad you stayed. That you love the way it feels when I touch you."

She remained silent until he slowed his pace. Maya whimpered, her eyes pleading with him not to stop. That wouldn't do. He needed to hear it.

"Say it." He pressed his lips to her ear. "I need to hear the words."

"I love the way it feels when you touch me. Please, don't stop. It feels so—"

Her back arched and her hips lifted as he resumed the motion, forming a tight circle over the sensitive bud.

He slipped his fingers farther south, plunging them both inside her liquid heat while he continued caressing her with his thumb.

Everything about this woman was enticing. The warmth of her body. The way her full, round breasts shifted as she moaned. Her labored breathing. The scent of her arousal. All of it so tantalizing that he felt drunk with the power he wielded over her body. And he hadn't even entered her yet.

His shaft strained against his trousers, more than ready to rectify that. He curled his fingers, massaging her inner walls until she cried out. He found her spot. Liam intensified his movements, inside and out, until she flew apart, her walls tightening around his fingers.

Maya lay on her back, shivering and trying to catch her breath as Liam removed his fingers from inside her.

He hadn't lied about his skillful use of one hand.

Her head swam, and her heart raced. He climbed out

of the bed and stripped off every inch of his clothing. She swallowed.

Color me impressed.

Her fists clenched involuntarily at the thought of taking his length in her hand. She licked her lips and raised her gaze to his.

He leaned down and kissed her, then rummaged in the drawer of his nightstand. Pulled out a foil wrapper, ripped it open and sheathed himself.

"Stand up." His voice was gruff, his eyes hooded. She complied without complaint or question, standing as still as her quivering knees would allow. "Turn around."

She did. Liam slowly unzipped her dress, allowing it to pool around her feet. She sucked in a breath as he unhooked her bra and it drifted to the carpet.

"Take those off, too," he said, motioning to her silky knickers. His breath was warm on her neck. He stepped back, allowing her just enough space to do as he'd requested.

As she did, she bent deeper than necessary to accomplish the task. His appreciative moan sent a shock of electricity to her core, heightening her desperate need to feel him inside her.

Liam pressed his hardened length to her back and wrapped his arms around her. He squeezed her breasts. Pinched the stiff peaks. She swallowed a yelp as the tinge of pain translated to a flood of pleasure where she needed him most.

He slid one hand between her thighs, and an involuntary moan escaped her mouth. She writhed against him, her knees barely able to hold her up. Liam planted soft, deliberate kisses along her neck and shoulders. The scruff of his beard sensitized her skin and intensified the sensation of the light kisses, tiny nibbles and sensuous licks that followed. He squeezed her nipple again. This time she couldn't hold back her cry.

He turned her. Pressed his mouth to hers. His tongue crashed against hers as he palmed and squeezed her bottom. Her body trembled with anticipation as his thick length pressed into her.

Being here, doing this, might make her crazy or reckless, but it felt damn good. In this moment, there was nothing she wanted more than to feel him inside her.

Liam lowered her onto the bed and poised himself above her as he pressed her thighs apart. He gripped his shaft, the skin pulled taut, and pressed the head to her opening.

She couldn't hold back the deep sigh of satisfaction that shuddered through her as the delicious sensation of Liam filling her worked its way through her body.

Liam's eyes met hers, wide with anticipation. Her lower lip trembled.

So beautiful.

Even more now than yesterday because he'd gotten to know her. She was the kind of girl he didn't deserve, but he was bollocks-deep inside of her now. No turning back for either of them.

He relished the soft sounds emanating from her throat. The way her round breasts, with their dark peaks, bounced as she thrust against him. Everything about Maya was intoxicating. He wanted to make this last. To leave her desperate for him. His body trembled. He was losing focus. He had to ensure that she jumped off the cliff first.

Reaching between them, he glided his thumb against her slick nub. Stroked her wetness. She squirmed, her body tensing.

"That's it, Maya. You're almost there." His words were a throaty whisper as he stroked the taut bundle of nerves and thrust deep inside her. "I want to see every ounce of pleasure on that gorgeous face. Just relax. Let go."

Her body trembled, accompanied by sensual murmurs he couldn't quite distinguish. Tight and warm, her walls spasmed around his throbbing flesh, magnifying the wave of pleasure rippling throughout his body.

He sped up his thrusts, crashing against her inner walls. Her responsive sighs came louder and faster, driving him closer to the edge. Being buried so deeply inside her felt incredible. He wished to bloody hell there was no barrier between them. He cursed, his body shuddering, as he collapsed beside her; his slick, warm skin pressed to hers.

Liam draped an arm around her waist, cradling her body against his as he kissed her shoulder.

Game over. He won.

Yet, as he stared down into her brown eyes, only one word came to mind.

More.

Maya had shattered into what felt like a million pieces, her walls clenching around him as she called out his name. She'd scraped her nails down his back and gripped his naked bottom. Felt an exhilarating sense of power as she'd squeezed his length inside her. Watched the pleasure building on his face with each additional thrust. The way he cursed, then called her name, his body rigid. Ecstasy etched into his handsome features.

Standing in front of the mirror of Liam's master bathroom, wearing his T-shirt, electricity tingled down her spine. She'd never done anything like this. Sleeping with a man she'd just met. Still, Liam didn't feel like a stranger. He knew her, knew her body, in ways Carlos never had.

She'd spent a second night at the penthouse. This time in his bed, limbs tangled. He woke her with kisses on her shoulder, the scruff of his beard grazing her skin.

Even now, her skin tingled in the wake of his kisses. His lips had explored what felt like every inch of her flesh.

The sex had been amazing. She'd had her fun and three of the most exquisite orgasms she'd ever experienced. However, she had no delusions about there being anything more between them. It was time to go back to being Maya Alvarez, Sofia and Gabriella's mom.

Playtime is over.

Maya emerged from his bedroom in her red strapless dress, lips pressed into an awkward smile. Her hair, damp from the shower, was shorter and curlier.

This was the point when he typically kissed a woman on the cheek, told her what a lovely night it had been and ordered a car service to take her home. Yet, he couldn't explain his need to see her again.

What part of one-night stand did he suddenly have difficulty comprehending?

"Maya, I'd like to see you again."

She regarded him curiously. "Didn't take you for one of those guys who promise to call when they know they won't."

"Quite right. I'm asking because I mean it."

She narrowed her gaze and searched his face. Lines spanned her forehead. "Why do you want to see me again?"

Liam laughed and scraped his fingers through his hair. "You aren't going to make this easy, are you?"

A wicked glint lit her eyes. "Where's the fun in that?"

"Well, I had a remarkable weekend with you. I'd like very much to do this again."

She rested her chin on her closed fist and smiled. "It'll be interesting to see what you do for an encore."

He reined in his grin. "Here's my card. Call me tomorrow. I'd love to see you again next weekend."

Chapter 8

Maya held her breath as Kendra slid into the booth at their weekly lunch date. She'd given her sister the basic rundown of her weekend and dodged any deeper questions. Easy enough over the phone. Seated face-to-face, with Kendra reading her expressions, it would be harder to downplay how the weekend liaison with Liam had affected her.

"It's been three days. Please tell me you called tall, dark and handsome." That was Kendra. Straight, no chaser.

Warmth spread to Maya's cheeks. She shook her head. "No, and I have no intention of calling him."

"Why not? You've been on cloud nine the past few days. I miss hearing that lilt in your voice. I know you do," Kendra teased. "You enjoyed yourself with him, didn't you?"

Heat flamed Maya's cheeks. She studied her menu. "Yes."

"So call the guy. Besides, when will you get another shot at banging one of the UK's most eligible bachelors?"

"What?" Head cocked, Maya sat taller in her seat.

Kendra smirked. "You really don't know, do you? I thought maybe he made you sign a confidentiality agreement or something, but you really, truly don't—"

Maya smacked the table harder than she intended to get her sister's attention. "Kendra, please. Just get to the point."

A wide grin spread across Kendra's face. "Don't know how to tell you this, little sis, but you got busy with a billionaire."

"I think you've got the wrong guy. Liam's in hospitality. He works for that new Pleasure Cove Luxury Resort going up on the beach."

"That's putting it mildly." Kendra practically snorted. "Westbrook International Luxury Resorts owns high-end properties on four continents and several islands. The company is worth well over a billion dollars. Pleasure Cove is just their fourth US property."

"Oh." She wasn't the only one who hadn't told the whole story about themselves this weekend. Not that his family's net worth was any of her business. In fact, it made her uncomfortable talking about it.

"You really didn't know this guy was super rich?" Kendra asked. "Didn't you spend the weekend at his place?"

"Yes."

"Didn't you notice—"

"That the place was expensive? Yes, but there weren't any gold-plated toilets or anything. Besides, his family is wealthy. That doesn't make him a billionaire. You've been reading too many romance novels."

"You're right. He isn't a billionaire. He's practically a pauper." Kendra smirked as she tapped out something on her phone. "His net worth is approximately forty million euros. Oh, and the guy is practically British royalty."

"You're exaggerating."

"I'm not. Take a look." Kendra turned the screen to face Maya.

Maya took the phone and scrolled through an article about Liam, complete with photos of the many starlets he'd dated over the years, including ballerina Karina Alexandrova and actress Carlotta Mayfair.

Maya's head felt light. Heat filled her chest. "I should've known they were lovers. There was something weird about the vibe between them. I was so starstruck over meeting Karina that I didn't give it much thought."

"You met her?"

"She was the lead dancer in *Swan Lake*. He took me backstage to meet her."

"He didn't take Karina home. He spent the entire weekend with you."

Maya didn't respond. The meeting with Karina replayed in her head. Had he screwed his old girlfriend right there in her dressing room while she was at the cast party?

"What's wrong?"

Maya groaned. "I wish you hadn't dug up everything you could find on him on the internet."

"Don't you want to know who you're getting involved with?"

"We aren't involved. It was a one-night stand."

"A two-night stand, technically," Kendra corrected, "and he asked to see you again."

"I was afraid seeing him again was a bad idea. Now I know it is."

"A bad idea? You must be joking. He's handsome, wealthy, generous…and did I mention wealthy? And he wants to see you again. What's not to love?"

"Look at the women he's dated. They're models and actresses and heiresses. Why would he want to be with someone like me? I'm not glamorous like those women."

"You're not a gold digger either. Maybe that's why Liam likes you. Because you aren't like any of them."

"Regardless of what else you might think of Carlotta

Mayfair, she's a savvy businesswoman and a marketing machine."

"Exactly. When a woman like that sees a guy like Liam, she's thinking corporate mergers and publicity potential. You're genuine. Open. Honest. Must be a refreshing change for a guy like him."

Maya cringed. *Genuine. Open. Honest.* She hadn't been any of those things with Liam. She hadn't lied to him, but she hadn't told him the whole truth either.

"Maybe." Even as she said it, she knew they'd both be better off if she didn't call.

"He asked you to call him. Gave you the power. Why aren't you using it?"

Maya shrugged. "It was a fantasy. Meeting a stranger and having one perfect weekend together. There's no point in ruining it by trying to make it survive the light of day." Maya propped her menu between them, blocking her face from her sister's view.

Kendra pushed the menu down so she could meet Maya's gaze. "Let me get this straight—your weekend with this guy was so amazing that you're afraid if you see him again it will ruin your magical memory of it?"

"So, you do understand?" She could use some reassurance that she'd made the right decision. That the misery she felt right now was worth it.

"I understand that's a load of BS. I'm just not sure if you're buying or selling it." Kendra cocked an eyebrow.

Heat filled Maya's cheeks. She dropped her gaze to the menu again. "It's the truth." Her voice felt small and weak. No wonder Kendra wasn't convinced. She sighed. "Of course I want to see him again. Last weekend was incredible. I haven't felt that way in forever."

"Now we're getting somewhere." Kendra rubbed her hands together and leaned forward. "You haven't felt what way in forever?"

Her sister was going to make her say it. Out loud. "Sexy. Beautiful. Vulnerable, yet powerful. I'd almost forgotten what it felt like."

"You and Carlos were like that, back in the day." Kendra's voice was low, her tone sympathetic. "I was envious of what you two had."

"In the beginning, we couldn't keep our hands off each other. After Sofia was born, things changed. Carlos didn't find me sexy anymore. I was the mother of his children. It was like there was this line he couldn't cross with me anymore."

When things had gotten stale between them, Maya suggested they spice things up in the bedroom. A chill ran down her spine as she recalled her ex-husband's cutting words. It had been more than three years, and still, the memory of those words caused the backs of her eyes to prick with tears.

No wife of mine is going to behave like some dirty whore.

After that, things continued to decline. More so after she'd gotten pregnant with Gabriella. Eventually, he sought what he needed, what he wouldn't allow her to be, with someone else. She sniffed and dabbed the corner of her eye with a napkin.

"I'm so sorry, Maya." Kendra squeezed her hand. "I didn't mean to dig up painful memories. But I wouldn't be a good sister if I let you go on pretending you don't have needs of your own. We cannot live by a battery-operated boyfriend alone." Kendra waggled her eyebrows.

Maya slid her hand from beneath her sister's and tossed a balled-up napkin at her. "I can't take you anywhere."

"You need me or you'd die a painful death of self-induced boredom." Kendra grinned. There was a quiet lull while they picked up their menus. After the server took their orders, Kendra studied her sister for a moment.

"Okay, I'm gonna say something, and I'm being one

hundred percent serious. So listen up." Kendra drew in a deep breath. "Honey, you're just afraid. Carlos hurt you. I get that. He isn't the only fish in the sea. You'll never find happiness in a healthy relationship if you're afraid to look."

"I have the girls and my work. That makes me happy. I'm not looking for another husband. My life is fine the way it is. Besides, if I was looking for a knight in shining armor, this guy isn't the one."

"Okay, maybe he isn't happily-ever-after material. So what? He made you happy, and you need some of that in your life. What's wrong with a little summer fling? With feeling the way he made you feel?"

"He'd never want me if he knew..." Maya dropped her gaze.

"If he knew what?"

Her face was hot. She leaned across the table, her voice low. "I didn't tell him I have kids. Believe me, there's no way this weekend would've happened if he'd known. The guy has confirmed bachelor written all over him."

"You really did go all in for the fantasy. I can't believe you managed to go an entire weekend without talking about Sofie and Ella." Kendra surveyed her sister's face.

"I didn't tell him initially because I didn't expect to ever see him again. He was staring at me like I was the most beautiful woman he'd ever seen. I was afraid he'd lose that fascination if he knew."

"Guess you've never heard of MILFs." Kendra raised an eyebrow, then laughed when Maya twisted her face in disgust. "He made you feel desirable. I get that. No judgment here. But why didn't you tell him later?"

"I tried, but he kissed me. I got caught up in the moment. Then we slept together, and it felt like it was too late to say anything, so I didn't. I didn't expect him to ask to see me again."

"Well, he did, so what are you going to do now?"

Maya traced circles in the condensation of her water glass and shrugged. "Don't know. It was fun. I'd like to see him again, but I'm afraid. What will he think when I tell him I'm not the hot goddess he thinks I am? That I'm just a divorced soccer mom?"

"Do you see this going beyond a few weekends of hot sex?" Kendra wasn't budging. She expected an honest answer.

"No. Nor do I want anything more. The guy doesn't believe in long-term relationships. It would be strictly physical. For the summer, maybe. Until the girls get back."

Kendra nodded. "If you're absolutely sure, and I mean unequivocally, I don't see why you have to ruin the fantasy. I'd love to say it won't matter, but in my experience, most guys lose interest once they know I have a son. They're terrified I'm looking for someone to take care of my child. It scares the shit out of them."

Maya squeezed her sister's hand. "You're going to find the right guy. Someone who deserves you and Kai."

Kendra smiled. "I know. Guess I have to kiss my share of frogs before I find him." They both laughed. The tension in Kendra's shoulders seemed to dissipate. "We're not talking about me right now. What are you gonna do?"

"You don't think I'm an awful person for not telling him?"

"The feminist in me says if he can't accept that you're a mom, forget him. As your best friend who knows you've been living like a nun the past three years, I say there's nothing wrong with a little summer fantasy lovin'." They both giggled. Then Kendra's tone turned serious. "If you keep this from him, it'll kill any chance of having anything real with him. Is that a risk you're willing to take?"

"My interest in Liam is purely physical. He feels the same way, I promise you."

Kendra smiled. "Sounds like you've already made your decision."

* * *

Maya stared at the same paragraph on her computer, laboring over how to start a fund-raising campaign letter. She was distracted and irritable. Angry with herself.

Kendra made it sound so simple yesterday. A little summer fling with Liam could be fun. Just what the doctor ordered. Still, as she sat last night, phone in hand, staring at Liam's card, all of those insecurities came back. The plain rectangular card simply stated his name and mobile number. No hint of who he was, or that his family owned a string of luxury resorts spread across the globe. Given his reputation, he probably had the cards made for occasions like this.

She lost her nerve and spent the evening watching reruns of *Girlfriends* while polishing off a bottle of Merlot. It wasn't as good as the wine Liam bought for her birthday, but it did the trick. For a few hours, she forgot how miserable she was without the girls and how much she wanted to be with him.

Now she sat at her desk with Liam's card peeking from beneath her keyboard. Taunting her. She'd promised to call the next day. That was four days ago. He'd probably hooked up with someone else by now. A woman who fit in his world. Someone like Karina.

Maya shoved the card underneath the keyboard. She needed to forget about Liam Westbrook and their weekend together. Besides, she had plenty to keep her busy, like working this funding campaign, planning their next event, and avoiding Kendra's calls and emails.

Her desk phone buzzed, alerting her to the intercom. It was the receptionist. "Yes, Elena?"

"Call for you on line two, a Mr. Westbrook."

She'd told Liam where she worked, and he remembered. Maya cleared her throat. "Thanks, Elena. Please put him through." She took a deep breath, her heart racing. "Mr. Westbrook, what can I do for you?"

He chuckled. "Back to that, are we?"

Maya shifted in her seat, her throat tightening. The sound of his voice and the auditory memories associated with it sent a shock of electricity down her spine and a steady pulsing between her thighs.

"I know I was supposed to call."

"Rather disappointed in you. Never took you for one of those women who says she'll call, then doesn't." His tone was only half-teasing.

"I intended to." She shifted the phone to her other ear and looked around to make sure no one had wandered near her office door. "I don't know. Seems like a bad idea, you and me."

"That's not how I remember our weekend together." She could imagine the wicked grin on his lips when he said it. The one she'd come to adore. "I had a lovely time. Thought you did, too."

"I did." She twirled the phone cord. "It's just… I'm not like the women you usually date."

"You've been consorting with Señor Google."

She cringed. "My sister Googled you."

"You can't believe everything you read, Maya." His tone was measured. "We were two people getting to know each other with the goal of having fun for one night. I didn't talk about my family or who I've dated because I didn't want preconceived notions to ruin that for us. Do you understand?"

Preconceived notions. Like the idea that a mother of two couldn't be sexy and desirable. A preconceived notion even her former husband hadn't been able to overcome.

"Yes," she said.

"Then I'd like to see you again this weekend, if you haven't any plans."

"I'd like that, but I need to be clear about something. I have no interest in a relationship. I'm not in a place where that works for me right now."

"I couldn't agree more. We would just be two adults enjoying each other's company and a bit of bloody fantastic shagging. No strings of any kind attached. Does that suit you?"

She reeled in the giddy grin she was sure he could hear in her voice. "I could think of worse ways to spend the summer."

"A summer fling, eh? Smashing." The confident, sexy grin returned to his voice. "Then I'm inviting you to my place for dinner tomorrow night."

"Sounds nice. What should I bring?"

"Dessert. Something spreadable. Oh, and an overnight bag. I don't plan to let you out of my sight all weekend."

Chapter 9

Maya inhaled deeply as the numbers on the elevator ascended. Two more floors before they reached the penthouse level.

Had she really agreed to a no-strings-attached fling with someone she barely knew? She had, but maybe that was what made it so perfect.

No intimate knowledge of each other meant no connections, no sentiments. Just pure, mindless, carnal pleasure. That was what she needed. Not the complications of a relationship. She'd work out her sexual frustrations over the summer then happily go back to her predictable life.

She glanced nervously at the concierge, who insisted on carrying her bag. He gave her a knowing smile and hiked the bag on his shoulder.

How many women has he escorted up this elevator?

The doors opened, and he gestured toward them. "After you, Ms. Alvarez."

She stepped off the elevator, but didn't move toward the door.

The man took pity on her and stepped up to the door, knocking twice.

When the door swung open, a savory scent drifted into the hallway.

"Thanks for escorting Ms. Alvarez upstairs, Andre." Liam stuck his hand in his pocket, peeled off a few bills and then stuffed them into the man's hand so quickly she might have missed it, had she blinked. He took the bag from the man. "I'll take it from here."

"Sure thing, Mr.… Liam." Andre tipped his hat and hopped back onto the elevator.

Liam folded his arms, the bag on his shoulder. "Still deciding whether to make a run for it?"

Maya stepped inside. "You're kind of a smart-ass, you know that?"

"I'm British. It's practically a national requirement." A small grin lifted the corner of his mouth. "Besides, you're pretty cheeky yourself."

She tucked her hair behind her ear and raised her eyes to his. "I need to apologize for not calling. I'm not usually the kind of person who says she'll do something and then doesn't."

"I realized that about two minutes into our first conversation. No worries. I'll let you make it up to me later." He winked.

She laughed, then stepped closer. He looked handsome in a pair of slim gray slacks and a light blue button-down short-sleeve shirt that hugged his muscular torso more tightly than necessary. The folded, buttoned cuffs accentuated his biceps and bronze skin.

No fair.

Her teeth sank gently into her lower lip at the thought

of sliding her hands underneath his shirt and tracing the lines of his well-defined pecs and abs.

"This is all new to me. I don't spend the weekend with guys I just met."

"That was clear about two minutes after we met, too. I'm just glad you're here." He closed the space between them and captured her mouth in a soft kiss.

A timer sounded from the kitchen. He sighed and kissed her again. "Hold that thought."

Maya grabbed her bag and followed him into the kitchen. She pulled out the dessert she made and put it in the refrigerator along with a can of whipped cream.

"Is that homemade chocolate mousse?" Liam put on a pair of oven mitts.

"It is. You like chocolate mousse I hope."

"I do." He looked far away for a moment. Liam cleared his throat, then opened the oven door. "My mum made it when I was a kid. It was my favorite thing in the world. She reserved it for occasions when I'd been a particularly good boy." He smiled wistfully. "Which wasn't very often."

"Is your mom… I mean, is she…" Maya stammered, shifting her weight from one foot to the other.

"Killed by a drunk driver when I was fourteen." His voice broke slightly. "Haven't had a chocolate mousse since."

The pain etched in the lines around his eyes broke her heart. Made her want to reward him in some way for the small vulnerability he revealed. Something she'd venture he rarely showed.

"Sorry about your mother. I didn't know. We can chuck the mousse. I'll run out and get something else." She adored her mother. They spoke by phone a few times each week. It pained her to consider a time when she'd no longer be part of their lives.

"No, I'm glad you brought it." His reassuring smile put

her at ease. He pulled a bubbling dish of lasagna out of the oven and set it on top of the stove.

"Smells incredible. Did you make it?"

"No, but I got the lasagna noodles off the top shelf for my housekeeper, Sarah, so she could make it. Does that count?" An impish smile returned the glint to his eyes.

"I don't know." Her eyes searched his. "Does it count that every day I didn't call, I wanted to?"

He nodded, pulling her into a kiss.

Liam sipped his café Americano, captivated, as Maya spooned another mouthful of mousse between her lush lips. The short belted dress she wore accented her delicious curves. Her shiny chocolate curls were swept into a low ponytail perched over one shoulder.

He managed to make it through dinner and dessert without stripping her bare and taking her right there on the table where they dined beneath the stars.

It hadn't been easy.

He'd done it despite the constant twitching of his knob, a natural reaction to her subtle flirtatiousness. If she licked that spoon one more time, he'd come undone. He was sure of it.

Maya was naturally beautiful. She wore only a hint of makeup and a colored gloss on her lips. The smooth brown skin of her legs and chest teased him, reminding him of what lay just beneath that little dress. She smelled divine. He'd barely been able to restrain himself from taking her to bed the moment she stepped in the door.

Now he sat with a large rectangular patio table between them, mesmerized by the smile that lit her face as she recounted a funny story about a coworker. The entire thing told in her melodic voice. Lyrical. Slightly husky. A hint of her Cuban roots evident just beneath her American accent.

She ate another spoonful of mousse. "You didn't hear a word I said, did you?"

"Sorry, love." He cleared his throat and put his mug on the table. "It's difficult to comprehend a single word coming out of that lovely mouth of yours while you're assaulting that spoon."

Her pupils dilated, and she licked mousse from her bottom lip in a slow, torturous affair that instantly increased the tension in his already-taut member.

"Got something against watching a woman enjoy herself?"

A flush of heat rose in his chest. Her confident, bold demeanor was even more of a turn-on than her innuendo-filled words.

"Not at all. I rather enjoyed it. Therein lies the problem. I'm a bit too taken with watching you enjoy yourself. All the blood in my brain has been routed elsewhere."

She came around the table and straddled his lap. The heat between her thighs grazed his length, and he let out a small groan in response.

"I see your point." The timbre of her voice descended to a husky whisper. "Must make it difficult to focus on anything else. Perhaps we should relieve you of any distracting thoughts."

Maya kissed him. Another groan escaped his mouth as she ground her pelvis against him. He dragged his mouth from hers, his breath ragged. A naughty grin perched on her lips, she dropped her gaze to his waist, loosened his belt and undid his trousers.

There'd been a shift in Maya's demeanor since her arrival. She'd peeled back the facade she presented to the world, unmasking a woman who was bold and uninhibited. She was a handful, and right now she had a handful of him. A ragged breath escaped his mouth as she squeezed his shaft. She stroked him, her thumb spreading the pearlescent droplets on his bellend. Their kisses grew frantic and hungry as she worked him with her hand.

His entire body trembled with a growing need to be inside her. He gripped her hand, though his body protested the interruption of a perfectly good hand job.

Liam pressed his lips to her ear. "I've fantasized all week about all of the ways I plan to tease that sweet little body of yours." She shivered in response. He slid the dress from her shoulder and laid gentle kisses at the juncture of her neck and shoulder. Trailed kisses up her neck. "And I don't want to wait another minute."

"Out here?" The look of arousal on her face gave way to distress. A sudden recognition of their visibility on the open rooftop at dusk and the lighting that was practically a spotlight.

He reached for the house remote, killed the lights on the terrace and dimmed the lights inside. "Better?"

Shoulders relaxed, she resumed her seductive smile. She traced his lips with her thumb, then pressed a kiss as warm and sweet as sticky toffee pudding to his eager mouth.

He pulled her closer, ravaging her mouth. His shaft stiffened, jealous of his tongue, plunging the depths of her mouth. Fumbling with the large belt at her waist, he unfastened it and tossed it to the ground.

Maya lifted her arms so he could pull the garment over her head. He tossed it aside, allowing himself a moment to take her in. His gaze roamed appreciatively over her curves, stripped down to a pretty pink bra and matching knickers. Liam tugged lightly on her ponytail, pulling her closer and kissing her again. He unhooked her bra, removing the barrier of lace shielding her perfect round breasts.

She trembled slightly against the cool night air. Gooseflesh arose along the warm brown skin on her arms. He dipped his fingers in the mousse left in his dish and smeared it on the tantalizing brown peak.

Maya inhaled at the sudden coolness on her warm skin. Her eyes fixed on his as he lowered his mouth over the pebbled tip and savored the sweet richness of the dessert, enhanced by the saltiness of her dewy skin. She threaded her fingers in his hair. Her grip tightened as he progressed from lazy little licks to ardent sucks and then gentle grazes of the swollen peaks with his teeth. He trailed kisses to her other breast, lavishing it with the same treatment.

He kissed her mouth again, hard and hungry, then shoved aside the dishes that were in front of him. He reveled in her response to his action. The small intake of breath that signaled her surprise. The elevation of her breathing. He gripped her waist, lifted her and planted her bottom on the table. He spread her legs, pushed aside the damp fabric shielding her slick sex and planted a kiss there before teasing the taut bundle of nerves with his tongue. She whimpered, her head falling back as she gripped the back of his head.

Liam pressed his hands to her abdomen, laying her across the table as he pulled her bottom to the edge. She exhaled deeply when he paused just long enough to drag the tiny scrap of damp fabric down her legs and toss it to the ground. The scent of her arousal mingled with the salty sea air.

She inhaled sharply, her muscles contracting, as he eagerly resumed his task. He loved the way her body responded. She was incredibly wet. Ready for him. Her face a mask of unbridled pleasure. Erotic and beautiful. His own personal *Venus of Urbino*. A sight that would drive any man mad.

A strangled moan fought its way past her sensuous lips. Lips he envisioned sliding along his taut, steely flesh. The thought of it sent a chill down his spine and straight to his bollocks. He anticipated ravaging her body, hearing his name on her tongue as she spiraled toward her release.

He increased the speed of his motion. Lapped at her slick, engorged flesh. Sucked her firm bud as she lifted her hips, her back arched. Breathy sighs and appreciative moans escaped her kiss-swollen lips, bringing him dangerously close to the edge.

She was sensual and beautiful, her face so expressive. Every ounce of satisfaction revealed in the gentle parting of her lips. The sensuous sounds emanating from them. All of it mesmerizing. He wanted to watch as she shattered to pieces, knowing he'd brought her such intense pleasure.

Liam plunged two fingers inside her, their movement matching the strokes of his tongue to her firm bud and the slick, swollen flesh around it. He was desperate to watch her spiral out of control, as he maintained his.

She gripped the edge of the table. Used the leverage to lift her hips forcefully against his mouth. Suddenly, her body tensed. Her walls clenched around his fingers as she uttered a string of Spanish words he didn't recognize. Then she called his name. There was no sweeter sound than Maya Alvarez calling his name in the throes of her release.

He wanted to hear it again. This time, while plunged balls deep inside her. He needed to hear the adorable sounds she made as the intensity of her climax built. To see the expression on her lovely face when she came, her walls clenching around him.

Liam pulled her onto his lap. She rested her head on his shoulder as she caught her breath. Her sex pulsed and her skin tingled, a current of energy running from her scalp to her toes. The prickling of her nipples was oddly delicious and painful all at once.

The way he'd tortured and teased her body, alternating pain and pleasure, had been nothing short of brilliant. He'd brought her to a remarkable release that left her blissed-out, yet desperate for more. And he seemed to derive as much satisfaction from doing so as he'd given her.

He made her feel desirable in a way she hadn't experienced. He didn't need to say the words. She saw it in his stare. She heard it in the low rumble to which his voice descended as his arousal escalated. She felt it as his fingertips traced her skin.

He wanted her, and she wanted him, too.

Maya lifted her head. "That was incredible."

"If you liked the opening act, you're going to love the full monty." His sexy growl sent shivers down her spine. He stood, setting her on her feet, then led her to his bedroom.

Maya lay in Liam's bed as he stripped and removed a foil packet from the drawer. She swallowed hard and bit her lower lip, her eyes following the subtle sway of his length as he moved.

She opened her hand, and he placed the foil square in her palm. Her heart racing, she tore the packet open and sheathed him. With a firm grasp, she slid her hand from the tip to the base. She raised her eyes to his again. They were filled with a desperate hunger that mirrored her own insatiable desire.

Liam lowered himself onto her, his gaze locked with hers. "I want to hear you call my name while that gorgeous body of yours is trembling with an orgasm. Knowing that every moan, every quiver, every curse, all of it, is for me." He nearly gritted out the words as he gripped his shaft, pumping it a few times before pressing it to her entrance.

Maya shuddered, her pulse racing. Every part of her anatomy responded to his gruff confession. Her nipples beaded painfully and the muscles low in her belly tightened. She wanted to touch him. To touch herself while he watched. To put on a show just for him.

She couldn't help the small sigh that escaped her lips as

he entered her. Nor could she hold back the whimper that followed when he pulled out again, teasing her.

Maya slid her arms down his strong back, her fingers tracing the tight, hard muscles. She gripped his firm muscular bottom, pulling him in deeper. He was fully seated inside of her, and still she wanted more of him. Every fantasy she had in the week since she was last in his bed flooded her brain. The things she'd imagined him doing to her. The things she wanted to do to him.

"Impatient, greedy little thing." His warm breath filled her ear. He pressed a kiss there and gently bit her neck. Enough to nip, but not break the skin.

She remembered his first words to her. *I don't bite. At least, not usually.* Maya tried to stifle a laugh.

"What is it?"

"You're not going to turn me into a vampire or something, are you?"

He grinned. "Or something. Don't worry. You'll like it." Liam nibbled and kissed her neck again.

She did like it, and him.

There was something about this man that drove her a little insane. When she was with him she could let go. Be the person she didn't dare allow other people to see. He was brilliantly adept at making her relinquish control. Slowly peeling away the suit of armor she wore in her daily life. The one that painted her sensible, practical, boring.

With Liam she could explore a side of herself she'd thought long gone. The uninhibited sensual being who enjoyed sex without apology. Who gave as good as she got.

She could be herself. *Almost.*

With Carlos, being a good wife and mother meant pretending she was no longer the woman who sometimes enjoyed being banged senseless. With Liam, she felt beautiful and seductive again, but it meant hiding the essence of who she was. Sofie and Gabriella's mom.

The difference was Carlos was her husband. He'd vowed to love her. All of her.

Liam had no obligation to her, and she had none to him, other than to bring each other mutual satisfaction.

"You okay, love?" He grazed her cheek with his thumb. "You're a million miles away."

She forced a tight smile, her cheeks warm. "Just wondering if you plan on teasing me all night, or—"

He jerked his hips forward until his cojones nestled against her bottom. He smirked. "You were saying?"

Before she could answer, he kissed her. His hips still in motion, his length reached the very depths of her, bringing her closer and closer to the edge.

"Me encanta, ay si, asi mismo." The words tumbled from her lips, without caring that he likely didn't understand them. Maya looked into his eyes. Whether he'd understood or not, her words turned him on. His dark eyes were hooded. His lips pressed into a taut line. Perspiration beaded on his forehead as he drove his hips back and forth. Maybe he did understand her request, if only instinctively.

Maya raised her legs, allowing him to go deeper. Intensifying the sensation of being completely filled by him. She dragged her nails over his firm, hard ass. Something primal in her relished the idea of marking him as hers, if only for tonight.

"Is this what you want, Maya?" His face strained with effort.

God, yes. Please. I want it. Now. She nodded, then pressed her mouth to his.

Liam knelt, his knees propped under her bottom. Lifting her legs, he braced them against his shoulder. He pressed soft kisses to her calf as he resumed his motion. His muscles tensed with determination.

The new position deepened the angle, the sensation delicious.

Maya clenched the bedding as she spiraled toward her climax, head light. She came hard like a truckload of bricks knocking her over a cliff. His name on her lips. A few more thrusts and his body tensed as he reached his pinnacle. Punctuated by a string of expletives. He fell into a sweaty heap beside her.

Liam pulled her against him and covered them with a throw. Still winded, he kissed her damp forehead. She wrapped her arms around him, shivering and speechless.

Neither of them spoke.

Tonight was perfect. Amazing sex. Nothing more. She could do this. Keep things strictly physical without the complications of a relationship.

She reminded herself of this every time he kissed her. Every time he was inside her. If she said it enough, eventually it would be true.

Chapter 10

Maya hitched her beach bag on her shoulders and adjusted her visor as she scanned the beach for Kendra and Kai. She spent most sunny summer Sunday afternoons at the beach with her sister and their kids. It felt strange to have the sun on her skin and soft, warm sand between her toes without the girls by her side. She waved and blew a kiss to her nephew, who stood at the water's edge. Kai waved back, squealing as the rolling surf splashed his legs and face.

Kendra sat beneath an umbrella, reading a novel. She slid her sunglasses down her nose and peeked over them. "Well, fancy meeting you here."

Maya unfolded her beach chair, placed it beside her sister's and sat. "You act as if I've abandoned you."

Kendra shoved her shades back in place. "I understand. We're just family. How could we possibly compete with a millionaire boy toy?"

"You're the one who encouraged this." Maya laughed.

"That's before I knew he planned to hijack all my weekend time with my little sis. Liam and I really should've discussed joint custody and visitation rights beforehand." Kendra grinned. "Where is he now?"

"On a plane. He has an early meeting at their LA office tomorrow."

"And how was this weekend?"

Maya's cheeks instantly tightened in a grin. "Spectacular."

Kendra adjusted her body toward her sister's, surveying her carefully. "You're glowing, you know that, right?"

"Feels like a hundred degrees out here. That's no glow, I'm melting."

"I'm serious." Kendra slid her shades on top of her head. "When I asked about Liam your face lit up like a Christmas tree. You do realize what this means?"

Maya shrugged, her right knee bouncing as she gripped the armrests of her chair. "That I like him? Obviously. It's a prerequisite to sleeping with someone. For me, at least." Maya regretted making the dig at Kendra's relationship with Kai's dad, Nate Johnston. Local boy turned NFL player. The man she still loved, but was too stubborn to admit it.

Kendra pursed her lips and folded her arms over her chest as she eyed Maya. "Thought this thing between you guys was strictly about sex."

"What do you think we've been doing?" Maya watched her nephew running along the shore with a little blond-haired boy he befriended moments earlier. Their arms were spread wide like airplane wings as they weaved in and out of the surf. She smiled.

"Then why does it feel like a lot more than that?" Kendra's question sent a chill down her spine.

Maya tried to look unfazed. "What makes you think it's anything more?"

Kendra pointed an accusatory finger. "That goo-goo-eyed gaze you had a minute ago? It's got star-crossed lovers written all over it. Call me crazy, but I'm a little worried."

"I love you, sis, but you're reading way too much into this. We've only been seeing each other a couple of weeks."

Kendra's voice was kind. "You're not falling for this guy, right?"

"Of course not." Her cheeks warmed when she realized how defensive she sounded. *Way to show he doesn't mean anything to you.* She cleared her throat. "We enjoy each other's company. That's all. Nothing to be alarmed about."

"Uh-huh." Kendra crossed her arms. "Look, Liam is handsome. He's rich. He's made you happier than I've seen you in a long time. So if there's more to this, I'm thrilled. But if you still haven't told him—"

"The plan hasn't changed." Maya's words came out more abruptly than she intended. She cleared her throat. "I appreciate your concern, but I'm fine. Stop worrying. Okay?"

"All right." Kendra's tone made it clear she wasn't convinced. Still, she knew Maya well enough to recognize this wasn't a discussion she was willing to entertain. Kendra glanced over at Kai, still playing with his new friend, then dropped her sunglasses back into place and picked up her book again. "Have you talked to the girls?"

Maya slumped against her seat. "I tried calling them on my way here. No answer. They're too busy having fun without me."

"To be fair, so are you." Kendra stared ahead, trying not to smile.

Maya hated it when Kendra was right. She only hoped she wasn't right about her developing feelings for Liam. Falling for Liam Westbrook definitely wasn't part of the plan.

Liam's heart danced at the sight of Maya beaming as she assessed herself in his bedroom mirror. She smoothed down the red fabric of the ball gown he'd surprised her with when he announced he was taking her to a gala for the reopening of the historic concert hall in Pleasure Cove.

The dress fit her like a glove. Maya lifted the hem of the dress to admire the red Badgley Mischka shoes he'd bought to complement the dress. A wide grin lit her eyes. "I can't believe you did this. This dress is amazing, and it fits like it was made for me. Thank you, Liam."

"You look stunning." He straightened his cuff links. "Besides, you're doing me a huge favor. I would've been bored to tears if I had to go to this thing alone."

The gala was a long-standing engagement he couldn't beg off. The Westbrook Charitable Foundation had donated a tidy sum to revive the concert hall. He was expected to make an appearance.

Liam hadn't intended to take a date to the event, but he couldn't bear to skip his evening with Maya. He'd become increasingly fond of her company, despite the temporary nature of their agreement.

He would've preferred to spend the evening alone with Maya in his bed. Still, bringing her along would make the night interesting. He'd make sure of that.

He led her down to the waiting limo. They'd been riding for all of ten minutes when Liam closed the divider separating them from the driver and pulled Maya into a passionate kiss. Her heart beat faster. Her skin prickled. Her desire for him pulsed deep in her core. All thoughts of how he was ruining her makeup and wrinkling her beautiful dress faded.

Liam slid his hand down the silky fabric. Over the pebbled tips of her breasts, down her side, then beneath the high slit of the dress. His hand snaked up between her thighs, nearly reaching its destination, before she had a moment of clarity.

Maya locked a hand on his forearm. "The driver will hear us."

Liam raised his hands in mock surrender, yet his eyes roved her body, exposing her in a way his hands couldn't. A chill ran down her spine and her cheeks grew warm.

He leaned in closer, his voice a husky whisper that tickled her skin. "I would never pressure you into doing something you don't want to do. But the thing is…I see you." He sat back with a knowing smile, his dimple on full display.

Maya ran her hands over her hair and shifted in her seat, already missing his warmth. "What's that supposed to mean?"

"It means I see the saucy little minx hidden beneath the prim and proper facade." He traced up her forearm, the touch as soft as a whisper. When she didn't respond, his smile deepened. "I see the woman who enjoys being a little bad—whose desires run as hot as a volcano, simmering beneath the surface, aching for release."

"I don't know what you're talking about."

"You can lie to everyone around you, love. You can even lie to yourself. But on some level, you know what I'm saying is true. I see that woman, and I'm inviting her out to play."

Liam's eyes danced as he lowered his mouth to hers. His insistent kiss stoked the fire slowly building deep within. Sent a jolt of electricity up her spine, malfunctioning her brain.

She should be mortified by his proposition. Yet, she was aroused by the prospect. Knowing the driver might suspect only made it more thrilling.

Sometimes it felt like he was inside her head.

Maya took a deep breath and straightened her dress, her eyes not meeting his. "Guess we'll have to see how the evening goes."

He chuckled. "Challenge accepted."

* * *

After mingling over hors d'oeuvres set out in the ornate lobby, they were given a tour of the space. The concert hall was adorned with Italian marble, lush fabrics, brass and etched glass. An intricate gold leaf pattern covered the ceilings overhead.

Nervous energy hummed throughout Maya's body. Every movement titillated her already sensitive sex and the pebbled tips of her breasts as they strained against the fabric of her dress. The featherlight touch of his hand on her back in the low-cut dress was driving her insane. Liam seemed well aware of this. He ran his hand down her back and arms at every opportunity as they toured the space.

Finally, they arrived in the ballroom where tables were set for dinner. She was supposed to be taking mental notes in preparation for her proposal to her boss about putting on a gala benefit for their organization. Yet, she was mesmerized by Liam in his element. The easy confidence he possessed was part of his infinite charm. He smiled and greeted a good number of their fellow attendees, then introduced them both. Networking was part of her job. But in this dress, at this event, she was out of her league.

Liam's lips brushed against her ear. "Stop fidgeting. You look gorgeous."

Maya lowered her hands from the waistline of her dress, where she was readjusting the satin sash. "Sorry, I'm a little nervous."

His fingertips glided down her arm. "Why on earth should you be nervous? You look incredible. You're making everyone here jealous."

"This is a very pretty dress," she conceded, as she smoothed the skirt. "If it weren't mine, I'd be jealous of someone wearing it, too."

"I'll bet their dates are even more envious. Who wouldn't want a woman as beautiful as you on their arm?"

Warmth spread across her cheeks as she held back a grin. "Flattery will get you nowhere, Mr. Westbrook."

"I disagree. I think it'll get me exactly where I want to go." He held out his elbow. "Come on, I want to show you something."

They left the ballroom and headed down a darkened hall toward the concert hall they had toured earlier. He took her down a back hallway and stopped in front of a ladies' room that was closed. He nodded toward the door. "It's in there."

"The sign clearly says—"

Liam opened the door and pulled her inside. He locked the door and pressed his mouth to hers before she could object further. When he'd finally given her a reprieve, she caught her breath, her heart racing. It was a beautiful bathroom, recently renovated.

"Is this where you disappeared to earlier?" She raised an eyebrow and poked him in the chest. He smirked, but didn't respond. "What, you thought you'd just bring me down here and have your way with me?"

He leaned in and nibbled on her ear, his breath warm against her neck. "Actually, I thought I'd bring you down here and let you have your way with me."

She laughed, but shoved her hands into his chest. "No way. We're going to get caught."

"Who else would come down here?" He wrapped his hands around her waist and kissed her neck. "Besides, the sign clearly says this bathroom is closed, and I've locked the door."

She was melting into a puddle of goo. Each kiss sent electricity along her skin. His hardened length pressed against her, increasing the dampness at her core. A small sigh escaped her lips as he thrust his tongue between them in a kiss that drained every ounce of her willpower. Her nipples were taut, desperate for his mouth. The rising heat and dampness between her thighs were almost unbearable. Of course she wanted him here. It was wild and a little dangerous. Everything she wasn't, but wanted to be for the summer.

"We have some unfinished business. It's been bothering me all night, and you've been tense and fidgety," he muttered between warm kisses to her shoulders and the tops of her breasts, exposed by the neckline of the dress. "I have just the thing to fix that."

He slipped his hands into the high slit of her dress and pushed her soaked underwear aside. A satisfied groan escaped his lips. "I'm not the only one who thinks this is a good idea."

She gasped as he strummed the sensitive nub. Knees shaking, she clutched his arm to steady herself.

Liam kissed her again, his kisses greedy and desperate. He continued to stroke her needy bundle of nerves, increasing the speed and pressure, bringing her closer to the edge. Abruptly, he pulled his hand away and tore his mouth from hers, leaving her breathless and longing for his touch.

His chest heaved, and his intent stare was reminiscent of a hungry lion sizing up his prey. He gripped her bottom, pulling her hard against him. "I'm going to shag you so hard that you'll want to scream my name at the top of your lungs until you're hoarse. But you can't. You'll have to hold it in. Can you do that for me, love?"

She nodded, holding his gaze. Her heart raced, her growing need for him palpable. Yet, so was the power she had over him. A dynamic that made her feel sexy and strong. It inflamed her desire for him. Her desire to do something so unlike her. "Quiet. Got it. Now shut up and unzip those pants."

His dark eyes clouded with lust as he turned her around

so she faced the mirror. He nuzzled her neck and slid the straps down her shoulders, exposing her breasts.

"Beautiful," he murmured into her ear as he lifted the back of the dress and pressed his hardened length against her.

He kissed her neck, unzipped his pants and slipped on a condom, pulled from his pocket. He teased her slick opening with the head of his thick erection before entering her with one quick move.

Eyes widened, her gaze met his in the mirror as she swallowed an involuntary groan at the delicious sensation of him filling her.

Liam seemed pleased with her unbridled reaction and entranced by the gentle sway of her breasts as he thrust into her. His expression contorted with the effort of his motion as he catapulted toward his crescendo.

One arm looped around her waist and held her firm against him. The other hand teased her hardened nipples with soft, steady grazes. He pinched one of the stiff peaks, creating a sensual blend of pleasure and pain that sent her careening over the edge into bliss.

She gasped, her walls clenching around his shaft as she clung to the counter to steady herself. Her legs trembled as a jolt of electricity made its way down her spine, into her belly and exploded deep in her core. She wanted to call out his name. To utter every obscenity she knew in English and Spanish. Instead, she pressed her lips together and breathed harder, a low keening moan escaping her mouth.

"God you're beautiful when you come." His breath came quicker as he gripped her waist and jerked his hips, increasing the speed and power of his thrusts. "Have you any idea how erotic those little noises you make are? How could I not want you? How could I not—"

His body stiffened and his length pulsated inside her as he came, calling her name softly, his lips pressed to her ear.

It was beautiful. He was beautiful. She didn't want him to let her go. Not now. Maybe never.

A foolish thought. One that had been creeping into her senses more and more lately. She forced a smile, then looked over her shoulder and planted a quick kiss on his lips. "We'd better get back to the party. You shouldn't have made such an impression. People will notice we're gone. What will they think?"

"I couldn't care less," he said, gruffly, kissing her neck. "I only care what you think, about what you want."

You. I want you.

The words, even uttered silently, surprised her. Sent a chill down her spine. Maya cleared her throat and slipped out of his grasp, desperately needing to put distance between them.

"I don't want to miss dessert. Or the auction." She straightened her dress and hair in the mirror, though she was careful not to meet his gaze.

"As you wish." Liam seemed disappointed, as if he'd expected a different response. He discarded the condom in a garbage bin filled with construction waste before heading to the stall.

Maya stared at her reflection in the mirror. Her hands shook.

No, no, no. She repeated the word in her head forcefully. *Do not fall for this man.*

It was a pointless argument. She already had.

Chapter 11

Liam stepped off Westbrook International's private plane and into a misty fog of gray rain. He hitched his leather knapsack on his shoulder and looked for the car his brother promised to send for him. His mouth turned to sawdust and a hard lump formed in his gut when he spotted the car, with Hunter leaning against it.

Squirmy bastard.

He should have suspected as much. His father's urgent request that they meet face-to-face was likely an elaborate ruse to trap him in the car with Hunter so they could talk.

Well, forget it.

Five years ago he'd boarded the same plane and moved to the US to put distance between him and his brother. He'd only returned to London a few times each year when business required it. They'd gotten through those years with minimal conversation. No point in changing that trend now.

Liam stalked across the tarmac, his eyes boring into his brother's. He wasn't the girlfriend-stealing bastard in this relationship. So why should he feel the slightest bit of discomfort?

His brother, who stood a few centimeters shy of his height, was leaning against a black company sedan with his arms crossed. The closer Liam got, the more Hunter resembled a man preparing himself for the full impact of a freight train. It was in those baby blues. The guilt. Hunter had never learned that his eyes said volumes more than his mouth, pressed into a harsh line, ever could.

"What are you doing here?" Liam crossed his arms and made a point of looking down at his older brother.

"We haven't seen each other in ages and still, you can't bloody well help yourself, can you?" Hunter lifted his chin, as if trying to add a few inches of height. Liam stared daggers at him, not responding. "You're my brother, Liam. We've barely spoken in five years. Doesn't that bother you in the least?"

Liam intensified his glare, making it clear it did not. "Why are you here?" He inserted a beat between each word.

Hunter ran a hand through his hair, ruffling his brown curls. "To welcome you home and bring you up to speed. Is that so wrong?"

A stabbing pain lodged itself in Liam's chest. He winced, averting his gaze from Hunter's. The man was daft if he believed that showing up here would suddenly put things right between them after what he'd done.

"You want to know what's wrong, Hunter? Stealing your brother's girlfriend. *That's* wrong."

"You conveniently forget that you and Merrie weren't together at the time."

Liam gritted his teeth and slipped into the passenger seat. His brother slid into the driver's seat and started the engine.

It was true, he and Merrie hadn't been together when

she'd taken up with Hunter. Still, as his brother, Merrie was off-limits. Any bloody idiot knew that. Besides, he and Merrie had been on and off since university. He loved her. If it weren't for Hunter's interference, he would have married her. Eventually. Perhaps had kids of their own by now.

His promises of someday hadn't been enough for Merrie. Tired of waiting, she'd given him an ultimatum. Either set a wedding date or walk away. He'd walked away, sure that once she cooled her heels she'd continue to be patient.

He'd underestimated her resolve. Merrie had been quite serious about moving on with her life. Worse, she'd chosen to do so with his brother.

They drove through the winding streets of London in ten minutes of glorious silence before Hunter spoke again. "I know you don't believe me, but I am sorry. Not about getting together with Merrie. She's the love of my life—"

"I'm sorry, do you imagine this conversation is making me feel better?"

Hunter cleared his throat. "What I'm trying to say is I'm sorry about how it happened. I'd never purposely hurt you, Liam. It couldn't be helped. For that, I'm very sorry."

"So in your mind there was a scenario in which you'd steal my girlfriend, and I wouldn't be hurt?" Hunter was dumbstruck, and rehashing old ground wouldn't help either of them. Liam steered the conversation to safer waters. "How's Dad?"

"He misses you."

"He's the one who sent me away, or have you both developed a convenient case of selective amnesia?"

"Father didn't send you away, Liam. You left of your own accord. We all understood why you chose to leave." Hunter's tone was contrite.

"I wasn't exactly welcomed with open arms when I was ready to return, now was I? He didn't even banish me to New York or LA, where I'd been. Instead, he sends me to some sleepy little Southern town, expecting me to pull off a bloody miracle."

Hunter winced, then glanced out of the driver's window. "We have great expectations for the Pleasure Cove property. Henderson wasn't working out. Who better to trust than you? You've done amazing things with our New York and LA properties. We need you to work a bit of your magic at Pleasure Cove. Make sure the property has a solid launch. Then you can handpick your replacement. It's as simple as that."

"Right. Seems more likely you thought I'd be too bored out of my skull to get into any sort of trouble. Happy to report that isn't true. I've found lots to keep me occupied," he said, thinking of the three incredible weekends he'd spent with Maya. She left his bed less than twenty-four hours before, and all he could think of during the plane trip was when she'd be in it again.

"Perhaps, but we haven't seen your mug splashed across the papers in months." Hunter smirked. Liam wanted to box his ears. "You'll be in London for less than a fortnight. Try to behave yourself, will you?"

A myriad of curses came to mind. He pressed his lips into a tight line and stared out the window instead.

Hunter pulled into a space in the car park of the Westbrook International office tower and tossed the keys to his brother. "Leave your luggage in the boot. It's yours while you're here."

"Thank you." Liam forced the words out in as civil a tone as he could manage.

"I must tell you one other thing." Hunter was on his heels.

Liam stopped abruptly, turning to face him. "Whatever it is, it's been written all over your face the entire ride here. Get on with it already."

Hunter took a deep breath and raised his eyes to meet

Liam's. "Merrie is eight months pregnant with our second child. A girl." His hushed words dripped with reserved joy and reluctant apology. "I'm going to be a dad again."

Intense pain gripped Liam's chest, making it difficult to breathe. As gingerly as Hunter said the words, he'd anticipated Liam's reaction. He'd be damned if he'd let the sod who stole the life he planned for himself revel in his devastation.

Liam shrugged, then punched the lift button. "Congratulations then, I guess." *There.*

"That means a lot to me. To us," Hunter stammered as they stepped onto the lift. "We wanted to tell you sooner, but I thought it best to tell you in person."

Heat flooded Liam's chest and neck as Hunter yammered on. Hunter had the girl he'd loved. The house and the kids. Now he was honing in on the business. The greedy bugger wouldn't be content until he'd taken everything.

Liam hit the stop button on the lift and dropped his bag on the floor. He shoved a finger into his brother's chest.

"I don't give a toss if you and Meredith have enough ankle-biters to form your own bloody team of footballers. I do care that you're trying to take my place in this company. If you think I'll sit by quietly and let that happen, you're completely off your rocker. I fight for the things I really want."

Hunter straightened his tie. "Dad built this company, and he's always believed you to be the right person to head it up when the time comes. I won't go against his wishes, whatever they may be."

He believed Hunter as much as he'd believe a bloody wolf that promised not to eat the sheep. Still, he was surprised Hunter hadn't swung on him. He'd always been a scrapper and he'd boxed for several years. Liam was the taller of the two, but Hunter was at least two stone heavier.

His brother could've easily taken him. Only one reason he wouldn't. The guilt must be eating him alive. *Good.*

Liam punched the start button then picked up his bag as the lift climbed toward the top floor, where his father kept his office.

"William, my boy, good to see you." Nigel Westbrook approached him, arms open.

Liam allowed his father, at least three stone lighter than when he'd seen him six months before, to engulf him in a bear hug. He hugged his father back, gripping his much-thinner frame. His cocoa-brown skin seemed a bit weathered and the wild gray hairs on his head and in his brows had multiplied. Liam's stomach sank. "Good to see you, too, Father. You've been well?"

"Well enough, my boy." Nigel patted his son's shoulder. "Glad you could make it. Your brother thought you'd refuse my invitation."

"Why? I'm part of this company, too, aren't I?"

Nigel's expression grew serious, yet he forced a smile. "You and Hunter are Westbrook International Luxury Resorts, son. Never forget that."

Liam kneaded the back of his neck. "As wonderful as it is to see you, Father, if you summoned me across the pond, there must be something important you wanted to discuss."

Nigel's glance slid to Hunter's momentarily before returning to his. "You're right, of course. I'd prefer to chat about it tonight, over dinner. I've invited Hunter, Meredith and little Maximus to join us. Thought we'd go to that place you like so much over in—"

"Father," Liam said abruptly. Nigel and Hunter stiffened in response. "Let's not pretend as if everything is fine between us. I've no desire to chat it up with the two of them. Whatever you have to say, I'd rather talk about it here. *Alone.*" He shot a scathing stare at Hunter.

Nigel cleared his throat and settled onto a nearby sofa.

"Very well, son. However, what I have to say concerns both of you, so your brother will stay."

"Fine." What choice did he have? He sat next to his father. "What is it that you couldn't tell me over the phone?"

Nigel stared at his hands, folded in his lap. The room was too quiet. The sinking feeling in Liam's gut grew.

"I told you I'd been a bit under the weather."

"You said it was nothing to worry over."

"And it isn't. It was cancer of the prostate." Nigel raised his hand in response to Liam's widened eyes. "There really is nothing to worry about, son."

"How on earth can you say that? It's bloody cancer. You could have…" Liam couldn't finish the sentence. Couldn't wrap his mind around the possibility.

"I say that with the utmost confidence because I've completed several weeks of external radiotherapy. My prognosis is good." Nigel smiled. "So any ideas dancing about your head of taking over the company are quite premature."

Liam was furious. Yet, his anger was mitigated by his concern for the old man. He couldn't bear the thought of losing him. "We've spoken nearly every week, Father. Why would you keep this from me?"

"Didn't want to worry you over such nonsense. I'm a warrior, son. A descendant of Nigerian kings and European conquerors. Never had the slightest doubt I'd pull through this like a champion racehorse." Nigel winked. "Bad enough I had to drag your brother and his family into it."

"So he knew, but you didn't bother to tell me." Liam glanced at Hunter accusingly.

Hunter's expression was apologetic. "I see him nearly every day, and we have dinner at Dad's most Sundays. He couldn't hide what was going on, even if he tried. I wanted to tell you, but it was Dad's choice. I had to honor his privacy."

"Meantime, I'm left out in the cold, as always. Mother would never have tolerated this. She knew how important family was." Liam clenched his fists.

"A lesson you seem to have forgotten, son." Nigel pressed a hand to his son's knee.

"You're making this my fault? Have you forgotten—"

"Of course not, but it's time you did. Time to put this petulant nonsense to rest. I know you were hurt, but you must let go of your animosity toward your brother and his wife. This isn't just about you or Hunter and Merrie. The future of our entire family is at stake. Do it for the sake of the family and the business."

Liam directed his angry stare at Hunter. "This wanker didn't give two shits about family or the business when he betrayed me five years ago. Why should I now?"

Not that he needed an answer from either of them. Their logic was shit, and he'd gotten the short end of the stick as usual. Hunter had always been his dad's favorite. It was his mum who had balanced the equation. His father's plan to name him as the next CEO was based on his business acumen and Hunter's lack thereof. Even that choice had only been about what was best for the business.

Liam picked up his bag and stood. "Forgive me, I'm suddenly feeling quite ill. I won't make it for dinner this evening. Breakfast at your place at seven?"

"If that's what you want, Liam," Nigel said to his son's retreating back. "But we will talk about this. All three of us. With the civility our family has always shown one another."

Liam's back stiffened. He turned back to them. "You're always so pragmatic in your approach to things, Dad. It's what makes you such a good businessman. But it's a bit like having Mr. Spock for a father. You're incapable of acknowledging my right to be angry. Of allowing me to deal with the enormity of what I lost. My brother and the woman I hoped to marry. Any man with half a heart and not so pragmatic an approach might find it difficult to come face-to-face with that betrayal every single day of his life."

His father stared at him, slack jawed and a little pale. Hunter hung his head.

"Don't worry. I'll be there for breakfast. We can have our merry little chat about the Westbrook legacy then."

Once he was alone on the lift, he checked his phone. There was a text from Maya, inquiring whether he'd arrived safely in London. Just seeing her name made him smile. He felt as if he could breathe for the first time since he'd arrived.

Chapter 12

Maya rummaged through the refrigerator at work for the box of leftovers from her dinner with Liam the night before: suya and jollof rice. He surprised her with a lovely meal at a local Nigerian restaurant—the only one in the area. The space was little more than a hole in the wall, but the food was magnificent. Liam said eating there reminded him of Sunday dinners at his paternal grandmother's as a child. The traditional Nigerian food was delicious, but she lost her appetite when Liam delivered his bad news.

He was returning to London.

Not forever. Just for the next two weeks. More important, he'd be gone for the next two weekends. She looked forward to their weekends together. Besides, the girls would be back in a few weeks, and this game they'd been playing would be over.

She tried to keep her expression neutral as he explained that he would miss their next two weekends together because of business. At first, she thought it was his way of breaking it off. Something in his eyes assured her he was just as disappointed.

"Come with me." His sudden request seemed to be as surprising to him as it was to her. "I'll be working most of the day, but we'll see each other in the evenings and on the weekends. You haven't been to London, have you?"

She must have heard him wrong. "Did you just ask me to come with you to London?"

He smiled. "I know it's last-minute, but you'll have a smashing time. Promise."

"You're leaving tomorrow night. I can't pick up and leave in an instant. I have a job. Responsibilities." The words spouted from her mouth rapid-fire before she could allow herself the luxury of entertaining his offer. She cleared her throat. "Thank you for the invitation, but I can't."

"You can't, or you won't?" His expression was serious, but his voice wasn't unkind.

Still, his question irritated her. He seemed incapable of comprehending how impossible it was for her to take two weeks of vacation at the last minute. But then, people who lived in Liam Westbrook's world did whatever they wanted, whenever they wanted.

No wonder the concept seemed foreign to him.

She wanted to say *yes*. To call in to work and tell them she'd jetted off to London for a fortnight, as Liam had called it. Hadn't she always dreamed of traveling to Europe? Maya swallowed the lump in her throat. Accepted the reality. Going wasn't an option.

"Can't." Her tone was firm but pleasant. "Thank you for the offer. Maybe next time…" Her voice trailed and her cheeks warmed. There wouldn't be a next time. The summer was quickly coming to a close. She forced a smile. "Bring me back something that screams tourist. Like one of those shirts that says, *My friend went to London, and all I got was this crappy T-shirt.*"

"Of course." The corners of his lips lifted in a smile that didn't quite reach his pensive gaze. "Then I suggest we not waste another moment at this table. I've every intention of ravaging that body of yours enough to sate us both until my return."

Maya remembered very little about the moments after that. What she did remember was being in his bed again and that the man was an absolute magician with that tongue.

Maya returned to her office with her leftovers and a soda. Her cell phone vibrated on her desk. *Speak of the devil.* Maya closed the door. "You arrived safely."

"I did indeed, beautiful." The smile in his voice made her go weak at the knees. She loved it when he called her that. Like he meant it. Okay, so maybe she was a little in love with that. What woman wouldn't be? "How's your day going?"

"Not bad, and yours? You must be exhausted after that long flight. Did you go in to the office?"

"Slept most of the flight, so I'm fine. Going in to the office, that was a bit draining. Headed to my flat now. Thanks for your message. Gave me a lift after a bit of bad news."

"What happened?"

The line was silent for a moment. "Nothing to worry about. Anyway, I've got to run. Just wanted you to know I've arrived safely. That, and I needed to hear your voice. I'll ring you in a few days. Take care, love."

What was it Liam wasn't telling her? Whatever transpired was obviously more serious than he was letting on. It hurt that he didn't trust her enough to tell her what was bothering him, but then why should he? She wasn't being straightforward with him either. Hadn't trusted him enough to tell him the most important thing about herself—that she was Sofie and Ella's mother.

* * *

Liam fixed himself a drink and settled onto the chaise longue. His head throbbed. The unconquerable Nigel Westbrook had cancer. Of the prostate, no less. It was unsettling in more ways than he could enumerate.

Despite the rows they'd had since the death of his mum, Nigel Westbrook had been his hero as long as he could remember. Even when he was an angry teen, acting out after the death of his mother.

His mum had decided to drive out to the country to spend some time with her sister. She was killed instantly by a drunk driver. The man walked away without a scratch. Meanwhile, Liam's family was left in shambles.

He wasn't that scared teenaged boy anymore, and perhaps he and his father weren't as close as they had once been, but he needed the old man just the same. Needed to know he was seated at his enormous desk on the top floor, even if it was an ocean away.

The doorbell rang and he sighed. *Hunter. Why can't you let it be?*

"I'm not in the mood for your apologies, Hunter." He swung the door open.

"Then perhaps you're in the mood for mine."

Liam stood dazed, nearly losing grip of the glass in his hand. As if seeing a ghost.

Meredith looked as though she might topple over at any moment. Yet she was beautiful. Even more than he remembered. She pushed her way past him and practically waddled into his flat.

Liam closed the door, his palm pressed against the wood, his back to her as he took a deep breath. He still hadn't spoken. Didn't know what to say. The ugly words he'd dreamed of uttering would make him a first-class arse. This woman was his sister-in-law, the mother of his nephew and heavily pregnant with his niece, which left nothing to say to her.

He opened his mouth to ask her to leave, but something in her eyes stopped him cold. She stood there, arms crossed. Anger and hurt dripped from her lovely gray eyes. A look he knew well. He sighed. As much as he'd once loved Meredith, he'd found no shortage of ways to disappoint her.

"I'd offer you a drink, but…" He shook the glass in his hand, then indicated her swollen belly.

"I don't need a drink." The shaky timbre of her voice indicated otherwise. "I need you to stop tormenting your brother. You hate me. I accept that. But Hunter's your brother, and dammit, he loves you. This is tearing him apart. I can see that it's tearing you apart, too. Why can't you just accept that Hunter and I are together? That we make each other happier than you and I ever could have?" Her false bravado quickly gave way as tears streamed down her face. She turned her back to him, her shoulders rising and falling with her sobs.

He'd always felt powerless in the face of her tears. He put his glass down and took a step toward her, then thought better of it. He bit the inside of his cheek and jammed his hands inside his pockets. Leaving five years ago had been wise.

"I'm not the one at fault here." His voice was quiet. He picked up his glass and took another sip of Scotch before taking a seat. "You have no right to come in here behaving as if I've somehow wounded you."

She stopped sniffling and stepped toward him. "I'm sorry you were hurt, Liam. But Hunter didn't destroy our relationship. You did that. We were together off and on for five bloody years. I'd waited long enough. You walked away, and I fell in love with Hunter."

Liam wanted to deny her words, but it had been his inability to commit to the relationship that pushed her away.

They were still young, and he was focused on his career. Had she fallen for anyone but his brother, maybe he'd be happy for her.

But karma was a vindictive bitch with one hell of a right hook.

He raised his eyes to hers, his jaw tight. "I loved you."

She sighed, shaking her head. "You didn't love me, Liam. You wanted to possess me. Like one of your precious things you could play with and adore whenever you wanted, then place on a shelf until you could be bothered with it again."

He grimaced. "That isn't true."

Merrie's face softened with pity. "I shouldn't have discounted your feelings. You did love me in your own way, but I needed someone who would love me wholly. All of the time, not just when it suited them. I needed what I have with Hunter, and he needed me."

Her words cut like a blade inserted in his heart. He couldn't respond.

Merrie sat at the opposite end of the sofa and rubbed her back. "Liam, long before we were lovers, we were friends. Good friends. I miss that, and Hunter misses his little brother. We *all* miss you. Nigel, Hunter, me." She sniffled, tears flowing again. "Your nephew is nearly three, and you've never laid eyes on him." She patted her belly. "Our little girl will be here soon. We want her to know her uncle. To love him the way we all do."

He gripped the glass in his hand so tightly he feared it would shatter in his palm. He threw his head back and finished the Scotch before meeting her gaze. "I'll consider it. Now, you'd better get home. Hunter will be worried."

"But Liam—"

"I'll think about it." He shot to his feet, arms folded. "That's all I can promise."

She struggled to stand. He sighed, then offered her his

hand, drawing her to her feet. The smell of her hair, like strawberries and sunshine, filled his nostrils. His chest tightened. Memories of that scent, and of him running his fingers through her sandy-brown hair flashed through his brain. He headed to the door with her trailing solemnly behind him.

Liam opened the front door. Meredith's determined gray eyes studied his carefully. She squeezed his hand before he could object. "You look well, Liam."

His spine stiffened. He didn't return the gesture, but couldn't bring himself to pull his hand away. "So do you. Motherhood suits you."

"More than you know." She lifted on her toes, her hands pressed into his chest, and gave him a quick peck on the cheek. "I hope to see you for dinner on Sunday."

"I'll—"

"You'll think about it." She cut him off with the wave of her hand. "Just know there's a space for you at our dinner table. Always. You're family. We all love you very much."

His tongue felt like it was glued to the roof of his mouth with an entire jar of peanut butter. He didn't respond. He could barely breathe.

Liam closed the door behind her and headed for the bar to make himself another drink. If the entire two weeks were going to be like this he'd be needing a lot more Scotch.

Chapter 13

"Liam! My goodness, child. It's so good to see you!" Mrs. Hanson wrapped her arms around his waist, hugging him. She was a tiny sprite of a woman whose red hair was now mostly gray. As she smiled up at him, her green eyes were as vibrant as ever.

"Missed you, too." He wrapped an arm around her shoulders as he allowed her to lead him into the house. "Hunter's here already, I see." He tried not to cringe as he said the words, but Mrs. Hanson didn't miss much of anything. If medals were given for being perceptive, the old girl would be a lock for the gold.

"Liam…" Her voice had the warning tone he remembered so well from his days as a mischievous boy.

"I know. He's my brother, and I should forgive him." He held up a hand, not wanting to mar the pleasant memory of seeing Mrs. Hanson with another lecture.

"Merrie's a great girl, Liam, but you'd have made each other miserable. You did make each other miserable. It's why you two broke up so often. Great friends sometimes make terrible lovers, my boy."

Liam ground his back teeth and jammed his hand in his trouser pocket. *Did they all rehearse that line?*

"It breaks my heart to see this family crumbling to bits. I know you were hurt, but it's time to let it go. The power to fix this lies solely with you." He opened his mouth to object, but she cut him off with a raised hand. "T'aint fair, I know. Life rarely is. But it's the right thing to do. We never regret doing the right thing, love." Not waiting for a response, she headed toward the kitchen.

Liam took a deep breath and stepped inside the breakfast room, where his father and brother were seated.

"Morning, son. Glad you could join us."

As if I bloody well had a choice.

"Morning to you, Father." Liam slipped into a chair on his brother's side of the table, leaving an empty seat between them. He nodded in his brother's direction. "Hunter."

"Liam." Hunter's voice was tentative.

"How was the drive out this morning, my boy?" his father inquired.

"Peachy." Liam drummed his fingers on the table. A few moments of uneasy silence settled over them. Hunter fidgeted like he was trying to crawl out of his skin. Liam couldn't take it anymore. "Father, you said there was something we needed to discuss."

"Not until we've had a proper breakfast." Nigel gave him a warm smile. "Why don't you tell us how things are going at Pleasure Cove? I'm sure Mrs. Hanson will eventually bring us breakfast." He cast his voice in the direction of the kitchen.

She hissed from the kitchen. "Hold your horses. I'll be there soon enough."

Liam chuckled. The two of them had gone on like that for as long as he could remember.

"Very well," his father said.

As if he had any other choice.

"I believe you were going to bring us up-to-date on the goings on at Pleasure Cove." His father looked at him expectantly.

Liam gritted his teeth. "Things are going well, as I've outlined in my weekly reports." His response was terse. He was in no mood for his father's stall tactics. "I thought I'd been rather explicit in them."

Nigel narrowed his gaze, trying his best to hide his annoyance. "You were. But that was company speak. The kind of thing that keeps the board and investors happy. I want your insight, son. That's why I sent you there. You have a sharp mind and keen powers of observation."

"I thought I was sent there because there isn't enough room in the sandbox for me and my backstabbing brother." Liam's fists tightened. He hadn't meant to say it. The words tumbled from his lips without a parachute.

"That's it!" Hunter scrambled to his feet and shoved a finger in Liam's direction. "I've had enough of this, you little shit. You and Merrie were over long before she ever had eyes for me. You're the only person who doesn't realize that. Maybe if you'd used those 'keen powers of observation' on the woman who loved you, you'd still have her."

In one swift move Liam was on his feet and landed a punch on his brother's jaw. He was so amped by the adrenaline in his system that he barely noticed the cracking sound and intense pain that immediately shot through his fingers. Instead, he felt a deep sense of relief. He'd been waiting for five bloody years to deck his brother.

Hunter stumbled back a few steps then looked up at him wearing an odd smirk. "There. Does that feel better? Or perhaps you'd like to sacrifice a few more of those fingers to your childish ego."

"You bastard!" Liam shoved the fingers of his undamaged hand in his brother's face. "How dare you make me the villain? This is about you stealing the woman I loved."

"That's exactly what I mean." Hunter shoved Liam's hand aside. "Merrie isn't a possession. You didn't understand that then or now. That is why you lost her. Not because I stole her away like a thief in the night. You left the bloody doors wide open and shoved her out of them."

Liam's breath came in hard pants. A jumble of thoughts clouded his brain. He ran his fingers through his hair and winced. God, he hoped he hadn't broken any of his fingers. He'd look like even more of an ass than he already did. "I need to get out of here."

"Liam, we are going to have this conversation this morning," his father said. "Step out for a few minutes to pull yourself together, if you need to, but I will not tolerate another second of this. If your mother could see you now. How disappointed she would be."

He felt like he'd been kicked in the gut. Worse, he deserved it.

"Hunter and Liam, both of you come with me to the kitchen. I'll get you some ice." Mrs. Hanson stood beside a rolling serving trolley that held their plates beneath silver warmers. Her expression dripped with disappointment.

Way to go, sport.

"I'm fine," Liam said.

"You say that as if it were a question." Mrs. Hanson invoked the familiar saying she'd used when they were lads.

"Yes, Mrs. Hanson." His usual response.

She unloaded her cart, carefully setting the plates on the table. Without a word she placed a gentle hand on Nigel's shoulder, so quickly Liam almost missed it. Just as he nearly missed his father's reaction to it. He took a deep breath, his eyes closing briefly.

"Come along, boys." Neither of them dared utter a single word of objection. She took out a clean dinner napkin and filled it with ice cubes, then handed it to Hunter. "Hold that to your jaw. Go on in and have breakfast with your father. He could probably use the company." Mrs. Hanson nodded toward the door.

"Sorry, Liam, but you needed to hear the truth." Hunter didn't wait for a response.

Mrs. Hanson shoved a bowl filled with water and ice cubes in front of him. Her lips were pressed into a straight line like she didn't trust herself to speak.

Liam slipped his hand into the cold water and winced. He moaned slightly as the sting of the ice reminded him how much his hand hurt.

"Serves you right. Thought I'd cured you of hitting others when you were ten."

He raised his eyes to hers, angry with himself for disappointing the one woman in the world who cared as much for him as his own mother. He was a first-rate ass for reasons that began well before he'd decked his brother.

"Liam, what's gotten into you? Fighting at the breakfast table in your father's house, like it's a common alley behind a pub. You should be 'shamed of yourself." Her words were firm, yet he could hear the pain in her voice. He'd let her down. He'd let himself down.

"I was disrespectful to you and to Father. Forgive me."

She sat beside him. "Thank you, but I'm not the one who deserves the apology."

Heat flared in his chest. "Father does, of course." He measured his words. "Maybe this wasn't the time or place, but Hunter got what he deserved."

Mrs. Hanson sighed. "Won't deny I wanted to deck him myself, at first. Once my anger subsided, I could see things more clearly. One day, I hope you will, too."

Liam focused on the ice floating in the bowl. "Hunter said I pushed Merrie away. That I treated her like a possession. Do you think that's true?"

"Doesn't matter what I think, love. Merrie is the one you should be asking. But it seems you believe there's some truth to it."

Liam shrugged, remembering Merrie's words. "Perhaps a little."

She gave him a tender smile. "Your brother was right, love. You needed to hear the truth. To understand what went wrong between you two. Maybe now you'll stop chasing every pretty girl that comes along, afraid of forming something real."

"It isn't fear. I've made a conscious choice not to get involved."

"You're afraid you can't trust your heart with anyone else. Maybe you're afraid of hurting someone the way you hurt Merrie."

His heart beat a little faster and his cheeks warmed. After all these years, the old girl could still see right through him. It was both comforting and unnerving.

"Time to stop hiding out in here while my perfectly divine corned beef hash gets cold." She took the bowl away and handed him a napkin. "You can't very well eat with this, now can you? I'll make you another once you're done. Now run along."

His father and brother ceased their animated discussion when he returned.

He settled in his chair and met his father's gaze. "I apologize for my behavior. That certainly isn't why I came here this morning."

"No." The disgust and frustration in his father's voice was evident. "You came here because I insisted. Otherwise, you wouldn't have had the civility to sit and have breakfast with your own brother."

Liam bit back the words he wanted to say. "For that, too, I'm sorry."

"Dammit, Liam! You've put me in a difficult position.

I hoped you'd be reasonable. That we could find an amicable solution to this dilemma."

"What dilemma?" Panic rose in his chest. He leaned forward. "Has something happened with Westbrook International?"

"Not yet." His father shook his head. "But I fear the fate of the company should something happen to me."

Liam didn't speak. He knew that look. Whatever his father planned to say next was as indelibly decided as Hammurabi's words chiseled in stone. He braced himself.

"You've got a clever head for business, Liam, and you've always shown the most interest in leading the company. But these last few years, you've put your own interests ahead of this company's. Ahead of the family's. That, son, will not do. Not for the man who is to be the head of Westbrook International."

Liam held his breath.

"I can't go on pretending as if I'll live forever. I must begin grooming one of you to take the helm. I thought I'd be handing the reins over to you, Liam. Your behavior these past two days confirms what I've long suspected. You cannot be trusted to do the right thing for the business if the choice is between doing that and spiting your brother." The words seemed to cause his father physical pain. He exhaled, then sat taller in his chair. "Therefore, I'm designating your brother as the next chief executive of Westbrook International Luxury Resorts. I'm sorry, son."

Liam exhaled, his head falling forward. "Can I say nothing in my own defense?"

"Whatever you might have said, your actions today spoke much louder." Nigel's voice was tinged with sadness.

"Hunter, I suppose this was your idea." Liam stood, buttoning his suit jacket. "If you'll both excuse me, I don't have much of an appetite anymore."

"Hunter had nothing to do with this." His father's voice

boomed behind him. Liam froze in his tracks, glancing over his shoulder. "He begged me to have this meeting and explain the gravity of the situation to you before I made my final decision. Your brother didn't take this position away from you, Liam. You've forced my hand."

Liam swallowed and headed for the door. He didn't bother saying goodbye.

Chapter 14

It was nearly seven thirty in the evening when Liam finished his final meeting for the day. He held his chin up and carried on as if his entire world hadn't come crumbling down around his ears. A performance that was mentally exhausting.

All the while, he couldn't get Hunter's and Merrie's words out of his head. Coming to terms with his culpability in the loss of Merrie had shaken him. To have that revelation closely followed by the loss of the prize he'd worked for his entire life—being named chief executive of Westbrook International—had knocked him completely on his ass.

Way to go, champ. You're a two-time loser.

He needed a stiff drink. After his long day, the last thing he wanted was to sit brooding on his sofa while he got shit-faced. He needed to get out and enjoy the vibrant London nightlife. Something he sorely missed. He rang up Wesley Adams, his best mate. After dinner and drinks, they headed to what had once been his favorite hangout, The Raven's Nest.

It'd been a few years since Liam had been to the club in London's West End. The crowd hadn't seemed quite so young then. He was reasonably sure the speakers hadn't been so loud either. Each bass note vibrated through his chest as if he were standing on one of the bloody speakers.

He glanced over at Wes, who seemed unbothered by the noise and crowd. His arms were draped around two giggling women at least a decade younger than either of them. His friend knew how to work that infectious smile of his. None of his charm was lost on the ladies surrounding him.

Liam stood with his back against the bar, sipping the last of his Scotch, when Wes caught his eye and waved him over. He nodded in acknowledgment, then turned back to the barman. "Another Scotch neat, please."

"I'll have what he's having." A tall, beautiful woman with what seemed like miles of smooth brown skin stood beside him.

He realized he'd been staring with his mouth open. His cheeks warmed. "Sorry to stand here staring like a complete tosser. You're a very beautiful woman."

She extended her hand and shook his firmly. "Brianna Evans. Pleasure to meet you."

"Liam Westbrook, and the pleasure is mine." He released her hand.

"The hotelier?" She surveyed him. "Thought you'd abandoned the UK for America."

"Abandoned is a bit severe, but yes, I'm currently based in the US. We're getting a new property up and running in Pleasure Cove. What about you, Brianna? What do you do?"

"Professional women's volleyball. As you can probably tell, I'm American. I'm here for a beach volleyball tournament with my partner, Rebecca Jacobs." She nodded toward a tall blonde woman holding court with a group of blokes.

The barman brought their drinks and Brianna reached into her purse to pay.

Liam asked the barman to add her drink to his tab.

"So, what are we drinking?" Brianna took a sip of her drink.

"Macallan 25." He smiled. "Is there any other Scotch?"

"I hope you don't think I'm going to put out just because you bought me an expensive drink." She cradled her glass. "Of course, Scotch like this might tempt a girl to fool around a bit."

Liam laughed, raising his glass. "And that is why it's worth its hefty price."

"To premium Scotch," she said, "and to meeting new friends."

They clinked their glasses. "Cheers."

Brianna was a beautiful girl. Intelligent. Funny. Effervescent. They joked that maybe they were too old and jaded to enjoy clubbing with coeds anymore. They talked about their work and the charity work she'd like to do when her career came to a close. An event she felt was just around the corner. The half hour they spent chatting allowed him to temporarily forget how royally he'd botched his future. A welcome relief.

Brianna stood and straightened her skirt. "Plan on holding up this bar all night, or would you care to join me on the dance floor?" She held a hand out to him.

He stared at her outstretched hand. The memory of him and Maya dancing the first night they met flashed through his brain. A twinge of guilt settled in his gut.

Brianna grabbed his hand and he followed her onto the dance floor. Liam slipped an arm around her waist and pulled her closer. The scent of coconut wafted from her dark ringlets. He settled into their movement, her body fitting against his. Guilt mounted in his chest, as if he were betraying Maya. Their first kiss replayed in his head. His body stiffened and his movements were off.

"What's wrong?" Her dark eyes searched his.

He grabbed her hand and led her to a remote corner of the club. "Look, Brianna, I'm seeing someone. It's nothing serious. I mean, that's what we agreed to, but somehow I feel… I don't know. I'm sure none of this makes sense."

"No, it does. Only it sounds more serious than either of you are willing to admit." She placed a gentle hand on his arm. "I think that's sweet."

"You're a stunning woman, Brianna, and I desperately needed a good laugh today. Can't thank you enough for that."

"And I needed someone to buy me a Macallan 25." They both laughed. "I hope everything works out for you. She's a lucky girl."

"Been looking all over for you, man." Wes approached, his eyes on Brianna.

"Wesley Adams, meet Brianna Evans. She's a—"

"Professional beach volleyball player." Wes grinned. His usual debonair smile had turned to a goofy, starstruck grin. "Watched your game earlier today. Wicked dig on that game-winning play."

A wide smile encompassed her lovely face. "Thanks, and thank you for watching."

Wes cleared his throat and stood a little taller. He seemed to regain his composure.

"Been following your career, even before you teamed with Bex Jacobs. Lived in England most of my life, but I'm American. I keep up with American sports as much as I can. There aren't a lot of African Americans in volleyball. I've followed your career closely."

"Wes is my best mate. We've been friends since boarding school." Liam nodded toward his friend, then added proudly, "He runs an event planning and promotions firm here in the UK. Works with a lot of high-profile clients."

"Pleasure to meet you, Miss Evans." Wes grasped her hand, his smile deepening.

"You, as well." She seemed as taken with Wes as he was with her.

"Brianna was my dance partner for the evening, but I'm knackered and about to head back to my flat." Liam put a hand on Wesley's shoulder. "I hate to abandon her middance. Would you mind?"

His friend's eyes lit up. He extended his hand. "Care to dance, Miss—"

"Bree," she said quickly, as she placed her hand in his. "And yes, I would." She turned back to Liam and smiled. "I hope you'll call your friend and tell her how you really feel about her." She winked at him.

"I knew it!" Liam heard Wes saying as they walked toward the dance floor. "The bastard's in love with her, isn't he?"

Liam shook his head and made his way to the door. Maybe Brianna was right. Perhaps he fancied Maya more than he was willing to admit. Still, what he felt for her was a far cry from love. Of that he was sure.

Chapter 15

Maya stared blankly at the television, wondering what the girls were doing. They seemed to be handling their summer-long separation far better than she was.

Kendra reminded her that she should be enjoying her time alone, but she missed the girls. She loved being a mom, despite the challenges of single motherhood. Sofie and Ella were the center of her universe, and she'd always been fine with that.

Being with Liam had knocked each meticulously aligned planet in her carefully constructed universe off its axis. Re-awakened parts of her she'd almost thought dead—her sensuality, passion and sense of self. All casualties of her failed marriage. When they were together she turned off her brain and her incessant need to be in control. She let go, free to explore her sensuality. She could revel in those feelings and desires, rather than being made to feel ashamed of them.

She'd given him control, yet emerged empowered, more confident. In the bedroom and in her everyday life.

A slow dread built in her chest whenever she thought about the end of summer. When it would be time to say goodbye. This was a short-lived fling, not a relationship. So why did she feel so guilty about the secret she'd been keeping?

She hadn't lied to him, and he'd never inquired whether she had kids. She simply hadn't volunteered the information. Still, she couldn't get her mother's words out of her head.

It's just as wrong not to tell something when you know you should, hija.

She groaned. Was Liam entitled to know everything about her? He certainly hadn't revealed everything about himself. She only learned he was from an obscenely wealthy family because Kendra Googled him. He'd been cryptic about the reason for his trip to England, too. When he called, she couldn't shake the feeling he wanted to tell her something. Something he wouldn't allow himself to say.

A familiar feeling.

Guilt ate away at her. She was keeping the most important part of herself from him.

Her phone rang. Maybe the girls were back from their aunt's. She picked up her phone and beamed. "How's London?"

"Peachy." His tone indicated otherwise.

"Liam, are you sure everything is okay?"

"Things haven't gone as I expected. Maybe I'm remembering everything through rose-colored glasses."

"Everything, like what?"

He sighed. "I don't know. Maybe I've gotten old, but a night out dancing just isn't as fun as it used to be. The music was too loud and everyone seemed so—"

"Young?" she offered, teasingly.

"I was thinking fake, but you're not wrong about the age difference. I felt like one of those sad old chaps who refuses to acknowledge his time has passed."

"Liam." Maya laughed. "You're being silly. You're only thirty-two. This doesn't sound like you. What's going on?" She folded a leg underneath her on the couch, straining to hear whatever it was he wasn't saying.

"Nothing," he said, after an achingly long pause. "Nothing at all."

It hurt that Liam didn't trust her enough to admit what was bothering him, but she had no right to expect full disclosure about his trip to London. Not when she wasn't being completely honest either.

She should tell him the truth.

Eyes pressed closed, Maya shook her head. Now wasn't the time. Whatever prompted his call had him down enough. She'd only make him feel worse. Besides, he deserved to hear the truth face-to-face.

"Liam, I know we haven't known each other very long, but I'm a good listener, if you ever need one."

"Thanks, I'll keep that in mind." He cleared his throat. "It's getting late and you've got work in the morning. I shan't hold you up. Just wanted you to know I've never enjoyed dancing with anyone as much as I enjoyed dancing with you." His voice was soft. Sweet.

She smiled, remembering their first dance. Their first kiss. "Me, too."

They said their good-nights and she got ready for bed. Her heart beat faster. Knowing that Liam was thinking of her, too, filled her heart with an inexplicable joy.

It'd been a long time since she felt that way about anyone. Cared for someone the way she cared for him. *Don't do this to yourself. Don't make this about more than it really is. Remember, this is just a summer fling.*

She paced the floor of her small bedroom, too wired to sleep. This fling with Liam was about sweaty tangled limbs and mind-blowing orgasms. Her heart was strictly off-limits.

Chapter 16

Liam cut his trip down to what felt like the longest ten days of his life. A shrewd man would spend the weekend recovering from the blow to his ego. Plot his next steps. But he could only think of one thing.

Her.

In the moments that felt darkest, thinking of Maya brought him back to the light. Memories of her vivacious smile lifted the heavy gray fog that hung over him. The sound of her voice, punctuated by her contagious laughter, alleviated the pressure building in his chest and enabled him to breathe again.

Since his return to Pleasure Cove, he counted the hours until he'd hold her in his arms. Hear the soft gasp that indicated she was close.

His excitement over seeing her warred with the tension that knotted the muscles in his neck and shoulders. His body was wound tightly from the stress of the past two weeks. Then there was the anxiety over how Maya would react to what he had in store for her.

Tonight he needed to be in complete control of her body. To please her in ways they hadn't explored. If Maya was willing to relinquish control, the experience could be incredible, taking what they shared to another level.

If she rejected the idea, or worse, was repulsed by it, it would likely signal the end. It was a risk. But if it paid off, it would be worth it for both of them.

Liam shook his head. He'd been staring at the door like a lovesick puppy eagerly awaiting his master's return. It was unlike him. No woman owned him.

So why was he behaving as if Maya did?

The buzzer sounded. Thankfully, he didn't have time to ponder the thought any further. He had much better things to do.

"Welcome home, Mr. Westbrook." Maya couldn't help the naughty smile that twisted her lips as she stepped inside Liam's penthouse.

Liam didn't object to her formal address. He kissed her cheek then made his way toward the bar. "Can I get you something?"

Electricity skimmed along the surface of her skin. The fine hairs on the back of her neck stood in response to a sudden chill. Was it coming from the blast of icy air from the overhead vent, or Liam's cool demeanor? Maya wrapped her arms around herself, unsure.

Something in his gaze made her shiver. Having seen it enough, she recognized the look of hunger in his eyes. Of desperate want. This was something else. A hesitance. Apology? Definitely sadness. She pressed her palms to his chest.

"Is everything okay?"

Liam tensed under her touch, then took the slightest step

back. He gave her a reserved smile followed by a quick kiss that felt like a whisper. Gone before she could be sure it was ever really there.

"London was great."

Her fingers drifted absently to her mouth. She cocked her head, taking him in. He looked emotionally spent. Something about the trip hadn't gone right, though it was clear he had no intention of discussing it.

"You look lovely." His voice pulled her out of her daze. He took her hand and led her to the sofa. "Glass of wine?"

She sat. "Please."

Awkward silence stretched between them as he uncorked a bottle of Cabernet Sauvignon. The knot in her stomach tightened and a burning sensation rose in her chest. Her breathing quickened.

Did he meet someone else in London?

It would explain the emotional distance he'd created between them. What they shared was temporary, and they never discussed exclusivity. Liam could see anyone he wanted. He didn't owe her any explanation, nor should she expect one. So why was there an ache deep in her chest?

Is it over?

If this was the end of their little fling, there was no point in dancing around it. Maya stood as Liam rounded the corner with her glass.

"Something wrong?" He handed it to her, one eyebrow raised.

"I'm not sure." She inhaled deeply, then took a generous sip. The wine was drier than anything she would've purchased for herself, but it had a deep, rich flavor. She let out a small murmur of pleasure.

Liam's nostrils flared and his pupils dilated. "Knew you'd like it." He sipped Scotch from his glass, then sat in the chair opposite her. "You were saying…"

She gulped her wine, then set her glass on the table. "This is goodbye, isn't it?"

He coughed. "Why would you think that?"

"You seem distant." She shifted her weight, not meeting his gaze. "Did you meet someone in London? Is that why you're so reserved? I know we never talked about this being exclusive, so you don't owe me an explanation." Finally, she studied his impassive expression, her heart racing. "Still, I'd like to know."

He set the glass down roughly and reached for her hand, pulling her onto his lap so she was straddling him. Threading his hands in her hair, Liam pulled her closer. His gaze locked with hers.

"You were spot on about my trip not going well. I'm a bit out of sorts because of it. It isn't you, Maya. The only thing that kept me sane during all of the madness in London was counting down the days until I came back here to you." He grazed her cheek with his thumb and smiled.

She tried to ignore the deep contentment that bloomed in her chest as she leaned into the hand that cradled her face. "Anything you want to talk about?"

"Not really." He cringed and shook his head as if the thought of it caused him physical pain. His hands drifted from her face. He lightly gripped her wrists instead.

"Maybe I should go. When I get like this I want to be alone, at least for a little while." It hurt to say those words. To think of separating herself from the warmth radiating from his body. "If that's what you want."

He tightened his grip on one wrist, almost painfully so, then loosened it just as quickly. His eyes met hers, his breath ragged.

"What I need is to be with you. Rough. Insatiable. Unapologetic. That isn't something we've done before, and I don't want to scare you off." He watched for her reaction.

She was silent. Not shocked, but more than a little surprised. His greedy gaze betrayed the sense of urgency that lay beneath his calm request and cool demeanor. Maybe she should've been terrified. Grabbed her things and got the hell out of there. Instead, what she felt was an indescribable sensation of heat like a lit flame, low in her belly.

Her brain told her to say *no*. That she wasn't the kind of girl who liked it rough. The warmth and wetness growing between her thighs revealed what her mouth wasn't willing to convey. The prospect of mindless, filthy, hot sex with Liam turned her on. Her nipples tightened painfully and her breath became shallow. She relished the thought of giving him complete control over her body while she turned her brain off and simply enjoyed it without excuses or apology.

Maya leaned in and pressed her lips to his, her tongue licking along the inside of his mouth, sucking the traces of Scotch from his lips.

Liam pulled his mouth from hers and set her on her feet. He stood and grabbed her hand, leading her to his bedroom. He nodded toward the bed. "Picked up something for you."

Maya picked up the red box tied with silver ribbon and shook it, trying to identify its contents. Finally, she turned to him. "What is it?"

He sat in a lounge chair in the corner of the room, his long legs crossed. "The first of several goodies I brought back from my trip." He tilted his head toward the master bath. "Go ahead and put it on."

Maya tucked the box beneath her arm and slipped inside the bathroom. Knowing Liam and what he'd said earlier, it could be anything. Fingers trembling, she removed the ribbon, opened the box and peeled back the layers of tissue paper. The nerves dissipated and she broke into laughter as she lifted the white T-shirt from the box.

"You remembered," she called through the door.

"That one's for you. Keep looking."

She looked beneath the T-shirt and smiled. *Yeah, that one is definitely for him.*

Lips quirked, Liam's dark eyes roamed her body as she stood before him. His heated glare raked across the stiff peaks straining against the fabric of the white cotton shirt with the words *My friend went to London, and all I got was this lousy T-shirt* emblazoned across it, bordered by the UK flag.

His gaze dropped to the underwear that was little more than a red silicone butterfly that housed a small bullet vibrator. Held in place by fabric straps, the panties covered… absolutely nothing. "Turn around." His low, gruff command went straight to her sex. Her body reacted with pulsating desire.

Maya complied, but glanced over her shoulder so she could watch his reaction. Tilting her hips, she gave Liam the best view of her backside, naked and completely exposed. She shuddered inwardly at the need she saw there. His pupils dilated and his lips slightly parted. The ridge of his length pressed against the fabric of his slacks.

Liam reached out to her and she stepped closer. He glided the back of his fingers up her thigh and pressed soft kisses to her hip bone. Guiding her onto his lap, he kissed her shoulder. "While I was in London, all I could think about was how it would feel to hold you in my arms. It's been a long time since…"

His words trailed off midsentence as he pressed his lips to her neck, then her ear. He didn't resume his thought.

Her chest tightened. She needed to know what he was going to say. Maya placed a hand on his cheek. "It's been a long time since what?"

Liam lowered his gaze to her mouth and traced her lower lip with his thumb. He shook his head. "Nothing, love."

She wanted to press further, despite the volatile mixture of anticipation and dread over what he might say. He pressed his lips to hers, stealing the words from her mouth, the breath from her chest. His kiss, hungry and eager, sent a shock of warmth to her core.

The hand at the back of her neck pulled her in closer as his warm tongue tangled with hers in a battle she was definitely losing. She was breathless. Her body vibrated with an intense desire for him. She was his willing captive, her only desire to please him. To soothe the pain he held inside.

Maya pulled out of his arms and sank to her knees, her eyes focused on the steely length evident through his slacks. She ran her hands along the ridge, needing to taste him. She wanted to give him the kind of pleasure he gave her. To make him forget what happened in London.

He seized her wrists. "Not yet, love." His husky whisper was a direct contrast to the message his body was sending. "I have something else in mind." He held up a small silver remote.

"Is that what I think it—" The words died on her lips as he pressed the remote, sending a shock of vibration to her core.

Liam stared at Maya. Watched as she hurtled toward bliss, soft moans emanating from her sensual lips. His length tightened painfully, aching to be buried inside her. His heart beat faster. He drew in a deep breath. Willed his body to behave. He'd know the delicious feeling of being bollocks deep in her soon enough. This was about giving her the ecstasy she deserved.

He would teach her that she didn't always need to be in control, while also feeding his need for it. Even if all he truly controlled was what happened between these walls.

Liam carried her to the bed and stood over her. Delighted in every twitch of her muscles, her warm brown skin glowing with a light sheen. The muscles of her abdomen contracted until finally she called out, pleading for a reprieve.

He granted her request.

She lay in bed, shuddering as she caught her breath, her eyes screwed shut. Liam reached into the dresser, pulled out a silk scarf and tied it around her head before she could react. Maya reached for the fabric.

Liam stilled her hands. "Relax, love." He knew how disorienting it was to be blindfolded. It could also be liberating, giving her leave of her inhibitions, making her more amenable to new experiences.

She was beautiful. Every inch of her. From her dark ringlets to her toes adorned with glittery red paint. Her chest heaved, the tight buds pressing into the fabric of the white T-shirt.

His body pulsated with a need to be inside her. To feel her soft, slick skin pressed against his. The way she squirmed beneath him as he took her from behind. He gritted his teeth and exhaled. There would be plenty of time for that later.

Liam reached beside the bed and pulled out the bag of naughty toys he'd bought. Heart thudding against his chest, his length strained in anticipation of bringing her to satisfaction in ways she'd probably never even imagined, his name on her lips.

Chapter 17

Maya awoke at seven in the morning with Liam's arm draped over her waist. He breathed softly in her ear. An involuntary smile tightened her cheeks. It was the first time she could remember waking to him still in bed. Liam went for a run at six nearly every morning, regardless of how late they stayed up the night before.

No wonder his body looked like an ancient Greek statue chiseled in marble. He was dedicated. Passionate. Driven. Always in control.

As he'd been last night.

She took a deep breath, trying to tame the flutters that rose inside as memories of the night before came rushing back to her. Last night she'd given him complete control of her body. This morning, she had the most delicious ache in places she would never have imagined. Had experienced things she'd only fantasized about.

The sex between them was passionate. Sometimes a little wild. She'd never felt sexier or as confident in her body, with all of its curves and dimples. She could let down her guard and explore her sexuality without fear of judgment.

He seemed to need the control she gave him last night, but she needed to relinquish control. He broke through her inhibitions and sent her spiraling into a heightened release that rocked her to her core. Something she wouldn't have achieved had she not given herself over to him completely.

Despite some slight bruising and a little soreness, nothing they'd done had made her uneasy. It was the words he'd uttered before he'd drifted off to sleep that had shaken her.

Liam held her as they both lay panting, trying to catch their breath, bodies beaded with sweat. He kissed her damp forehead and whispered, "Thank you, Maya. I needed that. I needed you."

The deep contentment she felt at his words and the gnawing sense that he meant it scared her more than anything he might have done to her body while she'd been blindfolded.

This was about hot, dirty, delicious "shagging," as Liam would say. Nothing more.

Suddenly, it was harder to breathe. She slipped from beneath Liam's arm, headed for the shower and tried to ignore the niggling feeling she had come to need him, too.

"What's all this?" Liam stood in the kitchen, clad in pajama bottoms. His dark hair was in a state of just-out-of-bed chaos. And those abs. So…lickable.

Maya shuddered internally at the visceral sensation of running her tongue along the ridges of his well-defined muscles. "Rather than ordering breakfast, I thought I'd cook this morning. I do have other skills, you know."

"Of that I've no doubt." He inched closer to the stove. "Smells delicious. What is it?"

"Chicken and waffles. It was a specialty of my paternal grandmother's. We always looked forward to brunch at her place." Maya smiled, handing him a plate.

"Chicken for breakfast? I have to say, it's a first for me, but it smells delicious." He kissed her neck. "I slept in for the first time in...I can't remember when...and now you're serving me fried food before noon. You're spoiling me."

When they sat down, Liam took a bite of the savory waffle and crispy chicken drizzled with her grandmother's special maple syrup recipe. He moaned.

Maya laughed. "I take it you like it."

"It's bloody fantastic," he mumbled through a mouthful of food. "A few more of these and I'll return to England two stone heavier."

She forced a smile and tried not to think of him returning to England or of their affair being over.

"Tell me more about this trip of yours. What happened while you were in London?"

He shrugged and chewed every bit of his food before responding. "It was business, mostly, but since ours is a family business, that requires dealing with family."

"It's good you got to spend time with your family. You said you have a brother and a sister-in-law. Do they have children?"

Liam's posture stiffened. "A little boy and my sister-in-law is about to deliver a little girl. From the looks of her, any moment now."

"That's exciting. Children are such a treasure." The words felt uncomfortable between them.

He shrugged again. "Not much of a kid person myself." From his reaction, she realized her face had fallen, matching the sinking feeling in her gut. "I'm not a kid hater or anything, if that's what you're thinking. Kids and animals are fine, I suppose. Haven't had much opportunity to find out. By choice. Even as a kid, my life was too busy for a pet."

"Of course." Hopefully, she hid her disappointment better this time. "Then it's good you don't have any kids or pets. By choice."

He smiled. "Indeed. If either of us had kids, we wouldn't be able to do half the things I have planned for us this weekend."

Maya took another bite. *Tell him. Tell him. Just tell him.* "Oh? More toys? Isn't there a limit on the amount of naughty things you can import into the country?"

He laughed. "I do have a few things I haven't broken out just yet. Didn't want to scare you off." He winked. "But I was thinking you might like to go skydiving with me this weekend."

She coughed, and the grapefruit juice she was drinking nearly shot from her nose. "Skydiving? Are you joking?"

"No." His response was matter-of-fact.

"Do I seem like the kind of girl who would want to go skydiving?" She should be flattered that he imagined her to be that brave.

"No, but you do seem like the kind of girl who'd love it, if you stopped obsessing about what you *think* you should do. Sometimes, the greatest pleasure comes in the moments when we lose control. Haven't I taught you that yet?" His enticing grin was an invitation to jump back in his bed.

"You're a pretty cheeky bastard." An increasing amount of British slang crept into her daily speech. Her coworkers had even teased her about it.

He laughed. "Doesn't mean I'm wrong."

He wasn't.

Skydiving was on her bucket list. As a teenager, she was a daring tomboy. She skateboarded and did crazy dance moves with her brother. She'd broken her leg climbing a tree because an older cousin said she couldn't.

Unfortunately, he'd been right.

Even when she and Carlos had married, she still had that

daring streak. That changed after they had the girls. She became a worrywart, constantly afraid something would happen to them. Carlos changed, too. He treated her differently. Even when it was just the two of them.

They stopped being fun.

When she tried to be adventurous again, even in the confines of their bedroom, Carlos's stinging rejection convinced her she was better off playing it safe.

Maybe she was wrong.

"It is something I'd like to try, but not any time soon." She caught herself before she said, *When my girls are all grown up and don't need me anymore.*

"What are you waiting for? A pensioner discount? C'mon, Maya. Live a little. Have you regretted a single thing we've done thus far?"

She shook her head. "No."

"Then trust me, you're going to love it." His eyes danced with excitement. Flashing that playful grin, there wasn't much he couldn't talk her into.

Still, she needed to draw a line in the sand somewhere. Here felt like a good place to start.

"Maybe we should start with something a little less daring. Preferably something that'll keep us closer to the ground." She took another bite of her food, relishing the tender juicy chicken and the savory waffle dripping with syrup.

"Fair enough." He winked at her, taking another bite of his food. "Tell me something else you want to do, but have been hesitant to try."

"Rock climbing. Or maybe zip-lining."

His eyes lit up. "I knew there was a daredevil in there. There's a place in Richmond, Virginia, I've been keen to try. We'll go next weekend, stay overnight. What do you say?"

"Okay. I'm in." Maya ignored the butterflies break-dancing in her belly, incited by a jumble of terror and excitement. "Now we can go back to what we were talking about."

"Which was...?"

She tilted her head, staring at him. "What happened during your trip?"

He became noticeably tense. "I appreciate what you're trying to do here. It's just not something I'm comfortable talking about right now. Not because it's you, but because I'm me. I've got my own way of dealing with things and *not* talking about them is right there at the top of the list." He sighed. "But thank you for trying."

Maya smiled. "Thank you for trying, too." He furrowed his eyebrows, a puzzled look on his face. "For pushing me to try new things," she clarified. "Can't remember the last time I've had this much fun. With a guy," she added.

"As opposed to a girl?" He wiggled his eyebrows and she laughed.

"Does every man have bisexual fantasies about his girl-friend?"

"Yes," Liam replied without hesitation.

They laughed, but then an uncomfortable silence settled between them. She'd called herself his girlfriend. That certainly wasn't what this was. Was it?

It couldn't be.

If she were actually his girlfriend she'd have told him about Sofie and Ella from the start. No, they were a summer-long one-night stand that got along especially well.

Simple as that.

She should tell him she misspoke. That she didn't presume to be his girlfriend. But that would only bring attention to the fact that she'd said it in the first place.

As if he hadn't noticed.

Judging from the uncomfortable way he shifted in his

chair as he ate, she'd venture that similar thoughts were spinning in his head.

Pretending it didn't happen would be best.

On Sunday morning, they ate brunch on the rooftop, taking in the beauty of the ocean and enjoying the warmth of the summer sun. Maya wore one of his shirts—a sight to which he'd grown accustomed. She looked comfortable and content. He was at ease having her there, sharing waffles and juice while breaking one of his biggest rules.

Maya was gorgeous. Sweet. More than he deserved.

Liam couldn't tear his eyes away from her mouth. Except when they roamed appreciatively over her curves. Nor could he resist the longing to be the one who set her laughter in motion. The crinkle of her eyes. The barely contained grin that began with the quirking of her tantalizing mouth. The way her perfect cheeks slowly hiked. The sparkle in her dark eyes. Then finally, the bubbly laughter so contagious he wished he could bottle it. If he didn't know better, he'd say he was in danger of falling for her.

He cleared his throat and stood, reaching for her glass. "I'll get you another."

"Thank you." She smiled, then continued her story.

Liam stepped behind the outdoor bar and poured himself two fingers of Scotch and another mimosa for her. Maybe the tiniest bit of distance would help him get his head back on straight. Stop him from marveling over her like an adolescent boy with his first serious crush. Yet, with each passing day, that feeling—a mixture of awe, deep lust, admiration and…affection—grew stronger.

He handed Maya her glass then took his seat. If he didn't find a way to rein his feelings in, he'd be putty in her hands, making it increasingly difficult to let her go.

But let her go he would.

It was what they agreed to. Now he just needed to get his heart and his other head back on board with the plan.

Maya sipped her mimosa, her eyes trailing down Liam's broad shirtless chest. Her gaze caressed the hard muscles, starting with his delts, then trailed the light dusting of hair that beckoned her imagination to dip below the strings tied at the waist of his pajama pants.

He cleared his throat. "Eyes up here, lady. Sometimes, I swear, you treat me like a piece of meat." A playful grin kissed his mouth.

"I lose my powers of subtlety after the third mimosa, so really, you only have yourself to blame."

Liam laughed. He put his glass down and pulled her onto his lap, trailing kisses down her neck. "Good, then my nefarious plan to get you tanked and make love to you all afternoon is working."

"Guess it is." She took another sip then put her glass down next to his. "But you didn't need alcohol for that. All you had to do was ask."

Maya unbuttoned the shirt she was wearing and left it hanging open as she leaned in and captured his mouth in a kiss. His warm, eager mouth took hers. Jolts of electricity skittered along the surface of her skin. She wanted him. More than she'd ever wanted anyone.

He wanted to make love to her.

That's what he said. Not shagging. Not having sex. Nor any of a number of crude American or British references he could have used. It was just a figure of speech. Not a promise. Nor an outpouring of emotions. Just an expression. She concentrated on the growing ache between her thighs and his swelling erection pressed against her sex.

Concentrate on the physical. Don't go reading between the lines, seeing stuff that isn't there.

She ground her hips against him and he moaned, the

sound vibrating in her throat. No matter what he'd uttered inadvertently, no matter what else she might be feeling, this was simply a summer of hot sex and good company. Nothing more.

She tried to push the voice from her head. The one that reminded her that the summer was winding down. Soon enough, this would come to an end.

Maya stumbled into her apartment on Sunday night exhausted. Her body still buzzed with sexual energy whenever she recalled the things they'd done. The trail of his tongue along her feverish skin. The salty taste of his. Despite the rug-burned knees, some sore muscles, and a few lingering bruises on her recently bound ankles and wrists, she felt incredible. It was a weekend of complete bliss.

Relinquishing control was intimidating at first, but he'd used that power to bring her indescribable pleasure. An eye-opening experience. At work and home, everyone counted on her to take control. She'd grown accustomed to it. Thrived on it. Sometimes, it was nice to sit back and let someone else take the wheel.

Maya winced, the tightness in her shoulders escalating, along with a growing sense of alarm. She and Liam weren't serious or exclusive and had no plans to be. So why did she feel so guilty that she hadn't told him about the girls?

She was living out some crazy fantasy she hadn't realized she wanted. But how could she keep such an important part of herself from Liam when they'd shared so much?

Maya shook her head. A brief snippet of how that conversation would play out rolled through her brain. He'd be shocked. Angry. Maybe even hurt. It would be over.

She wasn't ready for that. She needed to hold on to whatever this was until the very last moment. But soon, ready or not, it would be time to say goodbye.

Chapter 18

Maya had been quiet and pensive during the two-and-a-half-hour drive to Richmond, Virginia. She was pleasant, but tense, during dinner at the hotel restaurant.

When they returned to their hotel suite, he took her in his arms and kissed her. "If you don't want to do this, it's fine. We can find some other way to amuse ourselves this weekend."

"No, we came all the way to Richmond to rock climb." Maya shook her head adamantly and stepped backward. She exhaled deeply. Her shoulders relaxed, despite her nervous smile. "Besides, I want to do this."

"Do you?" He lifted her chin, studying her eyes. "Because I wouldn't think any less of you if you didn't."

"Liam—" she trained her gaze on his "—I'll be fine. It's just nerves, that's all."

"Then I've got just the thing to relax you." His smile widened.

She crooked an eyebrow. "I'll bet you do."

He laughed. "Not that—though I reserve the right to play that card later."

Maya shook her head, her arms folded. "What, then?"

He grinned. "It involves bubbles. That's all you need to know."

Maya's phone rang. She checked it. A genuine smile lit her face. When her eyes met his again, she averted her gaze. "I'm sorry, but I really need to take this."

He raised his hands, palms facing her. "Of course. I'll be in the other room. I should be ready for you by the time you're done."

Liam went into the master suite and closed the door behind him. Maya had taken a few other calls like that in the past few weeks. He'd wondered about who they were from, not that he had any right to know. Still, the change in her demeanor made him curious.

Stop acting like a jealous boyfriend.

Maya wasn't his girlfriend and whatever this was between them, no matter how good it was…it was only temporary. He shook his head and sighed.

Don't try and bullshit a bullshitter, mate. Maya's gotten under your skin.

There was no denying it. That only left one question.

What are you going to do about it?

Maya had gone down to the lobby to take the call from Sofie and Ella. On the way out to their aunt's for dinner, her little social butterflies barely had five minutes to talk. Maya made her way back to the room and let herself in. Guilt settled over her the moment she stepped inside. She hated keeping this secret from Liam. Yet, she couldn't bear the thought of how he'd react once he knew.

I'm not really a kid person. By choice. The words echoed in her head. "Liam?"

"In here," he called from the master bathroom suite,

where he sat in the spa tub—overflowing with bubbles. Soft strains of Poncho Sanchez's Latin jazz played from a portable Bluetooth speaker. "Saved a spot just for you."

Maya opened her mouth to object. Despite everything they'd done together in the past few months, the idea of taking a bubble bath together felt too…intimate. Like a couple in love on a romantic getaway.

His sincere smile halted her objection. It was a thoughtful gesture. How could she be anything but grateful?

"Thank you," she said instead. Maya undressed and slid beneath the bubbles. Liam encircled her in his long arms. She settled back, resting her head against his shoulder. The warm water melted the tension from her back and shoulders. She let out a contented sigh. "Brilliant idea."

He chuckled, the sound rumbling against her back. "I knew this would work. I know you better than you think, Maya Alvarez."

In many ways, he did. In others he didn't know her at all. She was to blame for that.

"Maybe a little." She held up her forefinger and thumb, leaving a sliver of space between them.

He trailed his fingers up her arm and kissed her neck. "*Swan Lake* and sappy commercials make you cry, but you don't want anyone to know it. You're fond of steak and lobster and you're far more adventurous—in the bedroom and out—than you'd like to let on. You adore your job because it allows you to give back to the community and make a meaningful difference in people's lives. You appreciate classic jazz because of your dad, but you're keen on Latin jazz because it's the perfect intersection of the two cultures that make you who you are. Not bad, eh?"

She stiffened slightly, shifting in his arms. They'd never discussed why she loved Latin jazz or the difficulties she'd experienced as a child straddling two cultures.

Liam instinctively understood her in ways she often

didn't understand herself. After the dissolution of her marriage, she was convinced she'd never find that kind of connection. She had that with Liam, only it didn't matter. What they shared wasn't real or lasting.

Tears pricked her eyelids. She cleared the lump in her throat. "What about you?"

"I'm an open book." He threaded his fingers through hers.

She ignored the implication that she wasn't being as open with him. "I know you like Nigerian food because it reminds you of your grandmother. Is it also an attempt to bridge the different cultures in your family?"

He shrugged. "I'm a classic mutt. I've got Nigerian, English, Irish and German roots. Never delved too deeply into any of my cultural roots except my grandmother's. Mostly because she was so proud of who she was and where she came from. She reminded my brother and me all the time that we should be proud of who we are."

"Sounds like an amazing lady." Maya couldn't help but smile.

"She was." He cleared his throat. "She was loving and kind, but she was also strong and determined—a real firecracker who wasn't afraid of anything. Gram is the one who pushed Dad to start his first resort. Even invested her life savings to help him get it started."

"Is that where you get your adventurous spirit?"

"That's where it began, for sure. Then I met Wesley Adams—the friend I told you about—at boarding school when I was thirteen. We hit it off straightaway. We're both competitive, so we're always trying to one-up one another when it comes to sports and such. Where anything else is concerned—anything that *truly* matters—we're nothing but supportive of one another. Always have been, right from the start. He's a remarkable chap. You two would get on well."

Maya clenched her jaw and held back the words that

almost rolled off her tongue. *I'd love to meet him.* She squeezed Liam's hand and inhaled. Now that her nerves had subsided, they could address the issue at hand. "What should I expect tomorrow?"

"To have fun. No pressure, at all."

"Okay, but am I supposed to just start climbing the wall? Aren't there things I should know first, like how to strap myself into the harness?"

"Of course. We'll get you into an early basic training class so you'll be comfortable with the equipment and learn some basic climbing techniques. If that's enough to satisfy you, we'll leave it at that. If you want more, we can try a few climbs."

Maya nodded. Her pulse elevated and her breathing became quick and shallow as she envisioned the towering climbing walls she'd seen on the gym's website.

"Hey—" he kissed the side of her face, his words as warm and soothing as the water she was immersed in "—everything will be fine. I'll be right there, and I won't let anything happen to you. I promise."

She exhaled, her breath coming in slower, steady streams. Liam would be there and everything would be fine.

Maya closed her eyes and tried not to think of what would happen in a few weeks when Liam would be gone.

She'd be anything but fine.

Breathe, Maya. Just breathe.

Maya stood, hands trembling, facing the thirty-five-foot-tall climbing wall dotted with colorful climbing holds of various shapes and sizes. The names of the holds cycled through her brain: jugs, pinches, crimps and slopes.

Look for the jugs. Avoid the slopes. Keep your arms straight. Don't forget to breathe.

She inhaled deeply, then released her breath, stepping

closer to the textured gray wall that seemed to mock her. Maya stomped twice on the mat below her feet, testing the padding. She yanked on the rope overhead, checked the double back buckle on her harness and tugged at the loose end of the double figure eight climbing knot securing the top rope.

Again.

Liam placed a gentle hand on her shoulder. He leaned down and spoke in a voice meant only for her. "You've got this, babe."

A tingle ran down her spine and into her fingertips. *Babe.* He hadn't called her that before now. She nodded and stepped forward, reaching out to grab the first hold—a wide purple jug hold two feet above her shoulder. She placed her foot on a blue hold with a wide edge and started to climb.

Straight arms. Grip with my fingertips. Pinkie toe and hip against the wall. Breathe.

She grabbed another hold and another, climbing higher.

"You're doing great, babe," Liam called from below. He'd chosen to act as her belayer—securing the other end of the rope and taking the slack from the line as she climbed.

Gazing a few feet above her, she kept moving, gripping one hold after another until she realized she was more than halfway up.

She froze, eyes squeezed shut.

Panic rose in her chest and her gut churned. She glanced back over her shoulder.

"Don't look down, Maya. Don't worry about where you've been, love. Focus on where you're going. You're almost there. Remember, you've got this, and I've got you. Just a little farther."

Maya nodded and opened her eyes slowly. *Breathe. Hip*

to the wall. Pinkie toe on the hold. Straight arms. Every-thing will be fine.

She reached behind her and dusted one hand at a time in the chalk bag at her waist. She blew on her fingers before reaching for the next hold, climbing higher and higher. The anxiety eased. Her trepidation gave way to excitement as the top of the wall came into view. Just a few more holds and she was there.

Maya squealed as she gripped the last hold. "Oh my God, I actually did it!"

"Never doubted it for a moment, love. Now hold on and I'll get you down." A wide grin tightened Liam's cheeks as he slowly lowered her to the ground. He was damned proud of her for conquering her fear.

"That was incredible! I can't believe I just did that." She jumped into his arms, laughing, the moment they were both unhooked from their harnesses.

"You were magnificent. Told you that you'd love it. Ready for lunch?"

"No." She pulled away, a glint in her brown eyes as she shook her head vehemently. Her curls, pulled into a top-knot, bounced. "We have to go again, at least once. You should go again first, though."

"Sure, if that's what you want." He'd been confident Maya would enjoy climbing if she allowed herself to relax and go for it. He hadn't expected to see that gleam in her eye. The one that signaled that she'd fallen in love with the alluring high of the adrenaline rush. One more thing they had in common.

He was more than a little turned on and in serious danger of falling for this woman.

"You know, if we get another staff belayer, we can climb together," she said, her eyes filled with excitement at the prospect. "I'll pay for the second one."

He wrapped his arms around her waist and dragged her against him, leaning down to whisper in her ear. "And miss the chance to watch you climbing the wall in those tiny black shorts again? Not a chance in hell, love."

"When you put it that way…" She giggled, batting her dark lashes as she raised her gaze to his. Maya lifted on her toes and pressed a soft kiss to his lips, her belly pressed to his length. "One more climb, then we'll have lunch back at the hotel. In bed." She wiggled her brows.

Liam's heart skipped a beat. Maya was smart and sexy, daring and adventurous. It had been a long time since he'd connected with a woman the way he had with her.

Yep, he was in serious danger of falling hard for Maya Alvarez.

Chapter 19

At five in the morning, Maya's heart beat frantically. She'd lain awake all night, her ear pressed to Liam's chest, listening to the sound of his heart—a sound she'd grown to love. She lifted her head, her chin pressed into his breastbone, and stole a glance at him as he slept. The man was beyond handsome. No wonder women like Carlotta Mayfair and Karina Alexandrova couldn't resist him. She reached out to stroke his beard, the hair tickling her palm. He stirred a little but didn't wake.

It had been an amazing summer, like something out of a dream. Liam was everything she wanted in a man. Confident. Strong. Handsome. Funny. And he wasn't put off by her strength. Nor was he afraid to take control. Each weekend she fell a little harder for him. Each Sunday evening it was harder to say goodbye, remove the glass slippers and slip quietly back into her normal life.

Maya choked back the tears that threatened to fall whenever she thought of this moment—one of the last they'd spend together. She'd always remember their time together. What he meant to her. He brought out a side of her she'd been terrified to explore, and she enjoyed every minute of it. Every second spent with him.

Their time together was supposed to be about pure carnal pleasure. She was filling a physical need with a man who could appreciate her mind and body. Who wouldn't censure her for her hidden desire to be adventurous in the bedroom. But the girls were returning from their summer in Puerto Rico the following weekend.

Playtime was over.

Time to return to her real life. Where her decisions were based on what was best for Sofia and Gabriella. Her needs didn't matter. Not when they conflicted with what the girls needed—a stable, orderly life.

Her traitorous heart wasn't content to play by the rules. Every moment they spent together her heart ached for him a little more. Wanted more than just his body. Because she was falling in love with him. A gross violation of the rules of their game.

Maya swallowed back the pain filling her chest and the tears that burned her eyes. A fling with Liam Westbrook didn't fit into the orderly, uncomplicated life Sofie and Ella deserved. So it was time to say goodbye. And she would.

No matter how badly it hurt.

Liam returned from his morning run, took a shower, then followed his nose to the kitchen, where Maya was busy at the stove. His stomach jumped for joy and his mouth watered, remembering the smothered pork chops, macaroni and cheese, greens, and sweet potato pie they dined on the evening before. His slacks fit more snugly, courtesy of her culinary skills. The very reason he ran an extra two miles.

"Smells bloody fantastic," he announced as he entered the kitchen.

She offered a smile that barely turned the edges of her mouth. Her eyes, which didn't meet his, held a pain he hadn't seen before. It made him uneasy. She handed him a glass of orange juice and he took a sip.

Maya finally raised her eyes to his. "I wanted to say thank you. This summer has been amazing."

"Sounds like a parting speech." The world stopped spinning for a split second. He surveyed her face. Her eyes, wet with tears, confirmed he hadn't imagined it. Liam's heart thudded against his rib cage. His mouth was dry, as if he'd swallowed sand. Panic rose in his chest, bitter and sudden like bile.

"Summer isn't over." He struggled to keep his voice unaffected, despite the feeling that his entire world had shifted.

"It is for me." She dropped her gaze from his.

"I don't understand. Have I done something to upset you?"

"No, of course not. We both knew this would end. What does it matter if we end it now or in three weeks?"

Everything.

He couldn't look at her. Couldn't stand to see the pain in her face, or to let her see the desperation in his. He needed her. It'd been a long time since he'd needed anyone. But he'd come to need the warmth of her skin. Her calming scent. The way her remarkable smile penetrated his armor and filled his chest with a feeling of incomparable joy.

It seemed the price one paid for that kind of need was disappointment. He cleared his throat. "I thought we had until the end of the month. I was going to surprise you. You said you always wanted to see London."

It was all the begging he could muster. After all, he had a modicum of pride.

She closed her eyes. A painful look crimped her delicate

features. She shook her head. The movement was slight, but the pained look on her face assured him she meant it.

"I can't. Please, try to understand."

"Well, I don't understand." He put the glass down and leaned against the counter, gripping the edge of the granite worktop. "Why didn't you say something before now? Before you decided this was over?"

He surveyed her face, needing her to see the pain he couldn't give voice to. Surely, she could see it.

The desperate need he felt for her wasn't just physical anymore. Little by little, they'd formed a deep emotional attachment. A precarious indulgence. One he hadn't allowed himself in some time. Not since he'd discovered the bitter truth. No one could be trusted. Not even your own brother.

Pain wrenched his chest. A pain he'd thought long gone. It gripped him like a dagger twisting in his chest all over again, reminding him not to lose his head over a girl he'd met only a few weeks before.

Maya was a fascinating woman, but hadn't he believed the same of Meredith until the moment she told him she'd fallen for his brother?

He'd gotten in too deep. Let Maya too close. Maybe it was best they both walk away before either of them could be hurt. Before he would let her walk away from him forever, he needed to be with her again. This time knowing it would be their last. He'd get his fill of her, and hope it would be enough to sate him of her forever.

He'd made love to Maya. Committed to memory the things he loved most about being with her. Her scent. Her soft curves. The desperate moans that vibrated deep in his chest and traveled down his spine. The lyrical phrasing of the Spanish she uttered at the height of ecstasy. The way she called his name.

He was utterly taken with this woman. Consumed with

a desire to be with her, in every sense of the word. The very thought that he might be falling for her caused an avalanche of emotions to tumble inside his chest. He was a confirmed bachelor. He loved his life and the freedom it afforded him. He could travel, take risks and see any woman he wanted without obligations or qualms of conscience.

So why was he allowing Maya Alvarez to turn his entire life upside down?

Things had gotten too serious between them. He'd sensed it for the past few weeks. He pushed aside those feelings and concentrated on the here and now. Now that Maya was abruptly ending their affair, he couldn't avoid them anymore.

He wasn't ready to let her go.

Liam held Maya in his arms, her face buried in his chest. Her breathing measured. She was quiet, emotional. If this was really what she wanted, why was she taking it so hard? If she didn't want to end it, why was she leaving?

There was something she wasn't telling him.

He'd sensed it early on, but he'd chosen not to delve too deeply. She'd tell him when she was ready.

Then again, why should she?

She tried to get him to open up to her about his trip to London. He resisted, preferring to keep his pain and family drama to himself. She was hurt when he refused to talk about it. Now he understood how she must have felt when he hadn't trusted her with his secrets. If he wanted her to open up to him, he had to be willing to do the same.

"I didn't want to talk about what happened in London because I did something stupid, and it cost me everything."

She propped her head on one hand. Concern etched between her brows. "What happened?"

He folded an arm beneath his head and groaned. "Got into a row with my older brother during a breakfast meeting with our father."

"A physical fight?" Her eyes widened when he nodded in response. "Why?"

"Before I left England, I'd been seeing someone off and on since university. I loved her, but she wanted a commitment. I wasn't ready to give her one. I walked away, expecting she'd be there, waiting, when I was ready. A foolish expectation, I know, but we'd broken up and made up so many times before. I thought it was par for the course. I was wrong. She fell in love with my brother."

"Your sister-in-law? That's who you were dating?"

He nodded. "I didn't take the news well. Seeing them together made me crazy. I needed some distance, so I moved to New York and started working with our new US-based properties."

"I understand why you were hurt, and I know you never really get over something like that." She tucked her hair behind her ear and lowered her gaze for a moment before meeting his again. "So the fight…was it because you're still in love with her?"

He shook his head. "My feelings went from love to loathing the second I learned the news. For the past five years, I've only dealt with my brother when business required it. I managed to avoid Merrie altogether. Until my recent trip. There she was standing in my flat, looking as if she'd pop at any moment. I couldn't look her in the eyes and hold on to the hatred I had for her. I realized I don't love her anymore, but I couldn't hate her anymore either."

"And your brother?"

Tension tightened the muscles of his face and jaw. "Certain lines you don't ever cross. I don't know if I can forgive him for that."

A pained look crimped her features. She lowered her gaze. "You said you lost everything because of the fight."

Tension filled his body as his father's words replayed in his head. "I won the fight, but lost the war. My father designated Hunter as the next CEO of Westbrook International. The one thing I've wanted my entire life."

"Because of the fight?"

"He feels I'm incapable of putting the interests of the family and the business ahead of my own." A deep pain expanded in his chest. "Maybe he's right."

"Liam, I'm sorry." The gentle hand she placed on his cheek soothed the burning in his chest. "I wish there was something I could say to make it better."

He brushed aside the curtain of dark tresses that shielded her face. "Having you here makes me feel better. Alive in a way I haven't felt in years. Maybe I am changing the rules, but I'm not ready to end this. Not yet. Neither are you. Why end things now, when everything is going so well between us?"

Her gaze didn't meet his. "It's not that I don't want to stay. I can't. I don't have room for this in my life right now."

"You mean you don't have room for me in your life right now." He dropped his hand from her face and stared at the ceiling.

"You don't know how hard this is for me. It has to be this way. Try to understand."

Liam folded an arm behind his head. He was hurt. Angry. Twice rejected. Unsuitable to be the next CEO of Westbrook International. Deemed unworthy of a real relationship with Maya.

So this was what the women he'd abruptly broken things off with had felt. He couldn't understand their hurt feelings over the breakup when he'd clearly set the expectations from the outset, and they'd agreed to it. Now here he was on the other side of the coin. They agreed to a no-strings summer fling. Then they would both walk away. He'd never expected that she'd be the one to call it quits, and that he would be the one gagging for it.

Karina had been quite right to call him an ass the day

she chucked that garbage can at his head. He was that and so much more. She deserved better.

He finally leveled his gaze with Maya's, Karina's last words to him running through his head. *And what about Maya? Can you give her what she deserves?* Liam swallowed hard. He couldn't answer that question honestly right now. Or maybe he wasn't willing to answer it. But he wasn't ready to let Maya go either. If that meant being the man she deserved, he was willing to try.

First, he had to ask the question that had been vexing him since her declaration that it was over.

"Maya, I have to ask you something. I need you to be completely honest with me."

Her body tensed. She worried her lower lip with her teeth but nodded. "Okay."

"Are you married?"

"Of course not." She bolted up in bed, pulling the sheet around her. "I would never do something like that. I know what it feels like to be on the other side of it."

Liam let out a sigh of relief as he sat up in bed, pressing his back against the headboard. "Sorry, I had to ask. I can't help feeling there's something you're not telling me."

A shadow fell across her face and she diverted her gaze. "Nothing I say will change the fact that this is over." She slipped from beneath the sheet and searched the floor for her bra and panties, then dressed.

He hopped out of bed, put on his boxers and came around to her side of the bed. "How do you know?"

Maya belted the sheath she slipped over her head and met his gaze. "Because I know you, better than you think."

"Try me." Hurt and anger rose in his chest. And, if he were being honest, fear. "What is it that you think you can't tell me?"

She raked her fingers through her dark curls, and then she raised her eyes to his.

"Why can't you just let this go? You've done this a hundred times before. Why is this so different? Because I'm the one walking away? Would it make you feel better if I let you call it off? Would that soothe your wounded male pride?"

"You think begging you to stay is good for my ego?" He clenched his fist at his side and released an exasperated breath. "Well, it isn't, and I don't care, because… because…"

"Because of what?" Her voice trembled.

He grasped her shoulders and pulled her closer. "Because I care for you. Because I've gotten quite used to you being around. I'm not ready to let go. I can't promise how things will turn out between us, but I'd like to find out. Wouldn't you?"

Maya's gaze dropped. She took a step backward, out of his reach, before returning her gaze to his. "I have two little girls. They've been away for the summer with their father. We're divorced," she added, probably in response to the gobsmacked look on his face.

He was speechless. He'd have been less surprised if she'd confessed she was a double agent who needed to leave for her next mission.

She powered forward with her confession. "They're four and five. Gorgeous, sweet little girls. I'm so lucky to have them, and I love them more than anything in the world. Sorry I didn't tell you sooner. This was supposed to be a one-night stand. But then it grew into something more and…" She palmed her forehead as she sought for her next words. "The closer we became, the harder it was to keep that part of myself from you. I wanted to tell you, but I was afraid of how you'd react."

Liam sat on the edge of the bed, his head in a fog. When she declared it was over, he felt as if he'd been stabbed in the heart. Her contrite admission set the blade afire and twisted it.

"So this entire affair has been a big lie." He struggled to keep his tone civil as he looked beyond her. Beyond the source of the piercing pain in his chest.

"I never lied to you, Liam, but I did intentionally keep this from you. It was wrong. I see that now. Back then, things didn't seem so clear. Neither of us wanted a relationship, so it didn't seem pertinent—"

"Bullshit, Maya. 'Omission is the most powerful form of lie.' You don't honestly believe that bollocks you're spewing, do you? Or is that your way of easing your sullied conscience?" His voice rose, hurt and anger roiling in his chest.

He'd appreciated that Maya was a mystery to be slowly unraveled, unlike many of the women he'd dated whose every move was subject to being reported by some rag or rabid blogger. She wasn't a mystery; she was a complete deception. She'd made a fool of him, and he'd let her.

Maya bit her lip, tears sliding down her cheeks. She wiped at them, angrily, with the back of her hand. "I'm sorry. I was wrong. But until today, you haven't been very forthcoming with me either. I accepted it because that's not what this was about. It was like stepping out of my own life and into a fairy tale."

"So everything we've done, everything we've been to each other... That was about fulfilling some fantasy of yours?" He bit the words out, his jaw tense, as he stalked across the room, away from her. "Glad I could be of service."

"It started that way, but for me, it became real. With you, I got to be the person there's no room for in my everyday life. You reminded me of who I once was. That there's more to me than just a soccer mom. I'm so grateful for what we've shared."

Liam turned toward her. Her face was wet with tears.

He fought the urge to take her in his arms and comfort her, as if he'd somehow wronged her. He clenched his fists at his sides. Quelled the hurt and anger building in his chest.

"You should've told me. I deserved to know."

She nodded, meekly. "I should have, but we both know the moment I told you, it would've been over. I wasn't ready for it to end." Maya gathered her already-packed bag and hiked it on her shoulder. She stepped in and kissed him softly on the lips. "Like I said, this is goodbye."

Liam didn't move. He didn't make an effort to stop her, nor did he allow himself the luxury of wrapping his arms around her and basking in the sensation of holding her close one last time.

Maya was right. They were done. How could he trust a woman who kept such a secret from him?

He stood in place, his feet cemented to the bedroom carpet, listening for the click of the front door.

There it was.

Just like that, she was gone. He should be glad. In a way, she was never really there. She'd been a dangerous illusion.

Maya Alvarez had a power over him no woman before her had. He was willing to give up his days as an unobligated bachelor and commit himself to her. Had imagined what it would be like for Maya to become an integral part of his life. Dreamed of waking to her lovely face and gentle laugh.

He was a fool.

At least now he knew the truth. He'd resume his life as it was before Maya stepped into it and changed everything. Liam locked the door. Then he crawled back into bed, hoping this had all been some awful nightmare. That he'd wake in a few hours with Maya by his side.

Maya punched the garage floor elevator button repeatedly, trying to force the doors to close. She needed to get out of there before she fell apart. The only way things could have gone worse was if Liam had thrown her out of his penthouse. He didn't raise any objections to her leaving, so the effect was the same.

She shut her eyes against the memory of the hurt and anger etched in his handsome features. He begged her to stay with him. To give a bona fide relationship between them a chance. Only to discover she'd been lying to him by omission all along.

Omission is the most powerful form of lie.

Her hands shook as she recounted Liam's acrimonious recitation of those words. Of course he was angry. She was a liar. A pathetic one who'd been taken in by her own lie.

She'd fallen for him a little more each week, but how could he possibly feel the same when she hadn't allowed him to see who she truly was?

The elevator dinged and the doors whooshed open at the garage level. Maya tossed her bag into the trunk of her car and exited the garage as quickly as she could.

She barely remembered driving back to her apartment. Once she was there, she flopped facedown on her bed and cried until she was hoarse, until her body was devoid of tears.

What did she expect? That he would open his arms and accept her after she'd kept this secret from him? He couldn't forgive his own brother. Not even when his inability to do so cost him everything.

Kendra warned her that any chance of a genuine relationship with Liam would be ruined if she didn't tell him the whole truth. She was right. Back then, Maya couldn't imagine that Liam was the man she'd want to spend the rest of her life with.

She'd been wrong.

None of that mattered now. She'd lost him forever, and that was exactly what she deserved.

Chapter 20

It was over. *Fine.*

It was a fling. A one-night stand that wouldn't quite end.

He should be happy Maya ended it. She saved him from himself. After all, he wasn't completely blind to what was happening between them. Gradually, what they shared became more than just sex.

It wasn't just her body he craved. He wanted all of her. To entwine his fingers in her luscious curls. The expressive smile that lit her eyes. The laughter that eased every ounce of tension in his body. Her sultry voice. And those curves. Liam closed his eyes, a slight chill running down his spine at the thought of them.

After he lost Merrie, he resisted the idea of giving his heart to any woman. Here he was falling for a woman who had two little girls. Being tied down by one woman wasn't appealing. Being tied to three was as appealing as being thrown into the Atlantic Ocean with an anchor tied around his neck.

Time to get over his hurt feelings and celebrate his fortunate escape.

"Fancy meeting you here."

Liam recognized the voice. He turned on his bar stool and scanned the tall, beautiful blonde who leaned one elbow on the bar as she stood between his seat and the next.

"Carlotta Mayfair. What on earth are you doing here? I thought you were working on a film in Belize or something."

"Ecuador." The edge of her mouth curled with satisfaction. "Keeping tabs on me?"

"Heard it in passing on one of those nightly entertainment shows." He tilted his head and took a sip of his Scotch. His gaze trailed to her lips, punctuated with a vibrant red that nicely contrasted her pale skin. "You haven't answered my question. What brings you to Pleasure Cove?"

She put her purse on the bar and climbed onto the stool beside him. "I'm guest starring in a few episodes of *The Islanders*. The show films here." Carlotta trailed her fingers up his arm, her eyes meeting his. "Must be fate. I've been thinking of you. More specifically, about those two weeks we spent in the South of France. Two glorious weeks with nothing to do. Except each other."

"A memorable holiday, indeed." Pure carnal fun on the warm sandy beaches. Most of it a haze of drinking, sex and a few other recreational pursuits. Yet, the memory didn't give him the satisfaction it once had.

Liam took another pull of his Scotch and surveyed Carlotta's face. She watched him expectantly. "If you don't have plans, would you care to join me for lunch?"

"Just here to pick up a quick bite. But you could buy me a drink, and later...who knows?" She flashed him the famous Carlotta Mayfair smile. The one that garnered five million dollars per film.

He motioned to the bartender. "A Sex on the Beach for the lady, please."

"You remembered." She grinned, leaning in to straighten his tie.

"How could I forget?" He turned back to face the barman, creating a bit of space between them. "And another Scotch for me, please."

"What brings you here?" Carlotta leaned back in her seat and crossed her mile-long bare legs. "Thought you were still in LA or that you'd have returned to London by now."

"We're building a flagship property in Pleasure Cove. I'm here to ensure things get off to a good start."

"I see. How long do you anticipate being stuck here?"

She'd said *stuck*, as if Pleasure Cove was a gray-walled prison. A conclusion he would have agreed with wholeheartedly when he first arrived. Now he felt at home here. Her remark jabbed. An insult to him and the place he called home, if only temporarily.

"Probably a year or so, but my stay has been rather enjoyable."

"Maybe I can brighten it a bit more." She leaned in—affording him a better view of her enhanced cleavage—and flashed him a salacious grin. "We'll be done filming tonight around seven. Why don't we meet for dinner?"

The barman brought out their drinks and Carlotta's carryout order. Then he asked her to autograph a napkin. Liam was glad for the distraction. He needed a moment to gather his thoughts. His first inclination was to beg off. There was a mountain of work on his desk. But that wasn't the real reason he was hesitant to accept her invitation.

One of the most beautiful women in the world, with the glossy magazine covers to prove it, was showing him nearly every square centimeter of her impossibly long legs. Yet, all he could think of was the woman he now considered the most beautiful woman in the world. It made him angry. Angry with Maya for lying to him. Frustrated with himself for wallowing in self-pity. He was pathetic. There wasn't a single reason for him to refuse Carlotta's offer. He could use the distraction of mindless sex. A sport at which Carlotta Mayfair excelled.

"Sounds splendid. Where did you have in mind?"

She smiled, then took a healthy sip of her drink. "Your place."

Liam didn't feel the glorious tightening of his slacks that a sultry Carlotta Mayfair invitation deserved. Instead, a wave of panic bloomed in his chest. He forced a smile. "Direct as ever."

"We're busy people, Liam. Who has time for that song and dance nonsense? We both know exactly what the other wants. That's the beauty of this on-again-off-again partnership we have. I can always rely on you to give me exactly what I want without any of the bullshit I don't have time for." She took a sip of her drink, looking pleased with herself.

Liam laughed. That's what he'd always liked about Carlotta. It was like being with the female version of himself. They understood each other perfectly. With her there was never any pouting when he was ready to move on. Nor had there been any real affection between them. It was simply about the sex.

Wasn't that what he wanted?

"Shall I pick you up at the set?"

"That'd be lovely. I'll text you the address." She took another healthy sip of her drink then stood, grabbing her purse and her lunch. She leaned in and let him kiss her on the cheek. "Until then."

Liam sighed as Carlotta strutted out of the restaurant, her walk still reminiscent of her days on the catwalks in Paris and London—where they first met. He had a sure-thing date with a gorgeous woman whose company he'd always enjoyed. Men would kill for his good fortune. He should be ecstatic. Instead, he felt slight queasiness with a side of guilt.

Damn that Maya Alvarez.

"Mami! Mami!"

Maya's heart leaped in her chest and tears stung her eyes. She'd recognize her babies' voices in a stadium filled with squealing little girls.

"Sofie, Ella! Mami missed you so much!"

Sofia and Gabriella jumped into her arms, nearly bowling her over. Maya wouldn't have cared if she ended up flat on her back with her feet in the air. Her girls were back home, where they belonged. She had enjoyed her fantasy summer. Pretending to be free and unattached. But *this* was who she truly was: Sofie and Ella's mommy. She peppered their faces with smooches as they giggled.

"Hello, Maya."

Maya let out a little sigh and climbed to her feet with the girls still clinging to her, as if they were afraid she'd escape.

"Carlos." Her voice was stiff, her jaw tight. Just a few minutes of polite conversation and then he'd be boarding that plane again and flying out of her life.

"Thanks again for allowing the girls to spend the summer with me and their grandparents. It meant so much to have them there for such an important event." His apologetic smile reminded her of how handsome he'd once been to her. "They made beautiful flower girls." He smoothed his daughters' hair.

"We have pictures, Mami. Wait till you see. Daddy, show Mami," Ella said.

"We can't hold Daddy up, girls. He has to board his plane home," Maya said. "He'll email us the pictures."

"But Daddy's spending the night with us, aren't you Daddy?" Sofie grabbed her father's hand.

Carlos cleared his throat. "If it's okay with Mami."

"What are you talking about?" Maya glared at Carlos, tension filling her muscles. She wanted to kill the man, right there at the Coastal Carolina Regional Airport, with her bare hands. "I thought you were flying back home to your precious new wife."

He stood a little taller. His gaze landed somewhere over her shoulder. "Staying over Saturday night makes the flight a lot cheaper. If it's a problem, I can get a room at a motel or something. But the girls begged me to stay with you... if that's cool."

"No, it is not cool." Her body tensed. Her head throbbed. She leaned in and lowered her voice. "What were you thinking to promise them a thing like that?"

"You know how persistent the girls can be." He shrugged. "I'm putty in their hands."

"The girls don't pay rent, Carlos. I do, and I don't want—"

"Please, Mami. Please let Daddy stay with us," Sofie pleaded.

Before Maya could respond, Ella had already joined in the plea. Their faces were so sad. It broke her heart. They spent the summer with Carlos, but before that they hadn't seen him in nearly a year. They wouldn't see him again until the holidays. She understood why they weren't ready to say goodbye to their father.

Maya clenched her teeth and breathed in deeply. They'd been divorced for three years, and he was still manipulating her. Worse, she was still letting him. He got exactly what he wanted while she sacrificed for the sake of the girls.

"One night. No more."

"Yay!" The girls jumped up and down squealing. They hugged her, then their father.

Maya leaned closer to Carlos, so only he could hear her. "Just so we're clear, know that this is the last time your sorry ass gets to pull some bullshit like this."

His eyes widened. He nodded, his expression solemn like a little boy called on the carpet when he thought he'd gotten away with something. "Understood."

Liam poured a glass of white wine and handed it to Carlotta. He grabbed his Scotch and sank into the sofa, leaving space between them. He turned toward her. His leg filled the void, making it less noticeable.

"Tell me about this guest part on *The Islanders*."

She raised a brow, head cocked. "You want to talk about my career?"

He loosened his tie. "Of course I do. Do you mean to say that—"

Carlotta put her glass down and laughed. "Did I offend you? I'm not sure I believed it possible."

Liam sat, stunned, cheeks burning. Is that what the women that floated in and out of his life believed him to be: an unfeeling monster? A few months ago that realization probably wouldn't have perturbed him. Now, it did. He'd been a callous ass. How could he not have recognized it? "Carlotta, I'm sorry if—"

"No need to apologize. We're two self-involved birds of a feather. That's why we get on so well, you and me. I'm perfectly fine with that. Thought you were, too." She slid the loosened tie from his neck and tossed it behind her. "I wouldn't ask you to change a thing about yourself, and I know I can expect the same." She pressed her lips to his.

He shut his eyes and tried to lose himself in the kiss, but the jumble of thoughts in his head wouldn't turn themselves off. Liam pulled away. His eyes met hers. "Sorry if I never showed any real interest in you before. It wasn't intentional. I was a bit preoccupied by this."

"*This* is exactly what you should be preoccupied with. It's simply an arrangement. Like a business transaction. There's no need to muck things up by pretending to care about anything else. Sorry if that sounds harsh, but it's true."

Liam gazed at his wristwatch and climbed to his feet. He ignored the miffed expression on Carlotta's face. "Dinner should be ready."

Carlotta's heels clicked on the hardwood floor as she followed him to the kitchen.

"Are you angry with me?"

"No, of course not. I thought it would be nice if we started the evening off with a proper dinner tonight, that's all. Maybe chat a bit." He peeked inside the oven. There were no flames and everything looked good. A few minutes still left on the timer. He closed the oven door. "You object?"

Carlotta sighed, her arms folded. She shook her head, begrudgingly. "Of course not, but it isn't necessary. Not between us. Because we understand each other."

Did they? Or were they both just so consumed with meeting their individual needs that nothing else mattered?

Liam led her back to the sofa.

"Good. We'll have a drink. Catch up. Have a lovely dinner. Then we'll go on with the festivities as usual."

"Sounds lovely." Carlotta forced a smile then took a healthy sip of her wine.

The food was magnificent. The conversation was decent. He coaxed Carlotta into the idea of dinner conversation. She'd been talking nearly nonstop since then. About herself. There was a moment when he debated whether she'd notice if he disappeared onto the balcony. He didn't, of course. Instead, he nodded politely and smiled long after he'd been bored stiff.

Once dinner was done, they were ready for the delicious trifle Sarah prepared for dessert. Liam gathered their plates and put them in the dishwasher.

"Haven't you become domestic?" Carlotta followed him into the kitchen.

"I'm loading the dishwasher. It's not as if I prepared the meal."

"Quite an improvement for you. I'm inclined to wonder who taught you that neat little trick. Remind me to thank her." A knowing smile turned the edges of her mouth.

His cheeks grew warm. He shut the dishwasher. "There. All done."

Carlotta wrapped an arm around his waist and pressed her body to his. "Time to move on to 'our usual festivities.'" She tugged him by his open collar and kissed him.

He encircled her waist, pulling her closer, but he felt... nothing.

His head wasn't in it. Worse, it was betraying him. Thoughts of Maya cycled through his brain. Her scent. The sound of her voice. Her taste—rich and sweet.

Then there was his body, which refused to cooperate. Just the sight of Carlotta strutting toward him, her eyes dark with lust, was usually enough to make his todger stand at full salute. But here she was, draped over him like a coat of paint, and he couldn't muster the slightest interest below his belt.

What was going on with him?

"You seem a little tense this evening. Hard week at work?" Carlotta yanked his shirt out of his trousers and slid her hand underneath it. Her fingers found his nipples. Teased them.

Still nothing.

"Got a lot on my mind." He tried to clear away the thoughts that were disrupting what promised to be a perfectly carnal evening. Even in her absence, Maya was cockblocking. Liam wouldn't stand for it. He needed to evict the thoughts of Maya Alvarez that had taken up residence in his brain. Carlotta was the perfect vehicle for such a mission.

So just go with it.

"Forget about work. At least, for now. Whatever problem you're stewing over will still be there tomorrow morning when I've gone. Now, kiss me like you mean it." Her nails grazed his skin as she resumed their kiss.

He looped his arms around her waist and pulled her deeper into him. Still, he couldn't shake the feeling of being completely detached. As if he were an observer, watching the entire affair with only the mildest interest.

There was a heaviness in his chest that hadn't been there before. What was wrong with him? He was with Carlotta Mayfair. Any man would kill to be in his position. Yet the only woman he wanted in hers was Maya.

Liam gripped her shoulders lightly and separated himself from her. She looked puzzled, almost hurt. "Carlotta, I'm sorry, but I don't think I'll be very good company tonight."

She tugged at his belt. "It's just stress. It'll be fine. I have just the thing for—"

Liam caught her by the elbows as she started to sink to her knees.

"No, Carlotta," he heard himself say, still not believing it was his voice. Was he really turning down a blow job from a woman who deserved an award for the vigor with which she approached the task? He'd either gone completely daft or… He swallowed hard and tried not to think of the alternative. Instead, he focused on the balls-up dilemma he'd gotten himself into.

Carlotta was furious. Her breath came in rough pants and her face was red. She yanked her arms from his grasp.

"Are you kidding me? You brought me here to…what, chat and have dinner? Was I not extremely clear about the one thing I had any real interest in?"

"You were quite clear. Forgive me, Carlotta. I would never have brought you here if I'd realized—"

"What? That you've suddenly become celibate?"

"No—"

"That you've got a girlfriend?"

"Yes. I mean…no. She wasn't exactly my girlfriend, and we're not together anymore." He rubbed the back of his neck.

"Then what is the problem? I'm here, and I'm willing. You must've been interested. You said yes." She folded her arms and paced the floor.

"When I said it, I meant it. At least I thought I did." He met her gaze, fierce and blazing. "I could feign interest and muddle through tonight, but it wouldn't be fair to you or to me. This isn't what I want. My interest…my heart lies elsewhere."

"But you're not together anymore."

"That's a mistake I plan to rectify." His voice was quiet. His heart beat frantically.

"You've changed." She narrowed her gaze, the words accusatory.

"I s'pose I have."

"I thought it only an urban legend, but apparently there are women capable of changing an intractable bachelor." She uttered the words with slight reverence. "You'll have to tell me her trick. In case I ever decide I'd like to tame a wily bachelor of my own."

"She didn't change me. Being with her reminded me what it's like to be truly happy with someone. One someone. I'd forgotten that." He kissed Carlotta's cheek. "It was good seeing you again. I'll take you back to your hotel now."

Carlotta's cold gaze softened. "She's a lucky girl. I certainly hope she's worth it."

He smiled. Maya was worth it. He only hoped she'd think he was, too.

Chapter 21

He rang Maya three times after returning Carlotta safely to her hotel. The first call rolled over to voice mail. The second and third went straight there.

Her message mocked him. *Do not pass go. Just go straight to hell.*

They had agreed to walk away and never look back. Now he was breaking their agreement. It couldn't be helped. He'd been daft to think he could walk away from her, that he would be okay going back to the way things were.

His unanswered calls indicated that Maya didn't feel the same. He couldn't accept that. He saw the truth in her eyes that day. She wanted more. Just as he did.

He had to see her again. If she was going to blow him off, she'd have to look him in the eyes and convince him that what they shared meant nothing to her.

A sudden heaviness squeezed his chest, making it

harder to breathe. What if he did mean nothing to her? Was he prepared to face the truth?

Liam turned off his idling car as he glanced up at her apartment. He'd waited until the next morning to visit her flat. Showing up at her door in the middle of the night wasn't the best way to convince her he wanted more than just sex. His legs felt heavy as he stepped out of the car.

He hadn't been this nervous since the first time he asked a girl out when he was fourteen. *Take a deep breath. Everything will be fine.*

A woman, hoisting a laundry basket on her hip, held the main door open for him. He thanked her and slipped inside.

Maya lived on the second floor. Right-hand side. He picked her up here when they spent the weekend rock climbing in Virginia. Taking the steps slower than a hundred-year-old pensioner, he finally stood in front of her door clutching an arrangement of amethyst-colored calla lilies and a box of truffles. He held his breath and knocked. No answer. He knocked again.

Please be here.

He honestly wasn't sure he had the nerve to make the trek a second time. Finally, footsteps shuffled toward the door followed by the sound of several locks turning. The door swung open.

The face peering at him wasn't Maya's.

"Sorry, I must have the wrong flat. I'm looking for a friend."

"Who's your friend?" The man, clad in an undershirt and a pair of boxers, crooked his brow, then leaned against the door.

"Maya. Maya Alvarez." An uneasy feeling rose in his chest.

The man frowned, deep lines spanning his forehead. He folded his arms over his broad chest. "You got the right apartment. Didn't catch your name."

"Liam Westbrook." He stood taller. "And you are?"

"Carlos Alvarez. Her husband."

Liam was sure his heart stopped. She said they were divorced. *Was that a lie, too?*

"My *ex*-husband," she said adamantly. "Who are you talking to anyway?"

"Your friend." Carlos turned in the direction of her voice.

She appeared in the doorway wearing a tank top and a pair of sleep shorts. Her eyes went wide. "Liam, what are you doing here? We agreed this was over."

"We were wrong."

"Is there a problem, Maya? You need me to—"

Maya spun around and pointed a finger at Carlos. "I need you to get dressed. Now. *Please.*"

Carlos grunted and sauntered to the couch where there were sheets and a pillow. He'd obviously spent the night on Maya's couch.

Liam sighed in relief.

Maya stepped into the hall in her bare feet and pulled the door closed behind her. She led him farther down the vestibule, away from the door of her flat. She quickly dropped his hand as if it were on fire. "You shouldn't have come here."

"I shouldn't have let you walk out that day," he said firmly. "Not without a fight."

"Liam…" She dragged a hand across her forehead. "What we had was amazing, but it's over."

He gently lifted her chin, his heart thumping against his breastbone. "Then look at me and tell me you don't feel anything. That what we shared meant nothing to you."

Maya pulled out of his grasp and let her gaze drop. "Of course it meant something, but I can't do this. I told you that from the beginning. You said this would be a summer of bloody fantastic shagging, no strings attached."

He cringed, hearing his own words thrown back at him, mimicked in his accent. "I know what we said." He put a hand on her shoulder. She bristled beneath his touch. "But everything changed for me. I thought it did for you, too."

She lifted her chin, her jaw tight and her arms folded. "Nothing has changed for me. I told you my life is complicated. There's no room in it for a relationship. Besides, we both know you don't like complicated relationships."

"That's not what I want anymore, Maya. I want you."

Her lower lip trembled, and her eyes were damp. Maya shook her head, and her curls, bound in a low ponytail, bounced over her shoulder.

Liam ran a hand through his hair and blew out an exasperated breath. "Can you honestly say you haven't the faintest desire to find out where this road leads?"

She stood taller, her tone resolute. "It ends here. Please, don't contact me again."

He could barely breathe, hurt and anger filling his chest. "If that's what you really want." He managed the words through a grimace.

Her expression softened and she took a step toward him. Lifting onto her toes, she kissed his cheek. "Goodbye, Liam." She turned and walked away.

"Wait." He caught her elbow. When she turned to face him, he thrust the lilies and the box of candy into her arms. "Consider this a final gift."

"I can't accept—"

"Then trash them." The words came out more clipped than he intended. "I've no use for them."

Liam barreled down the stairs and out the door, before she could object, leaving a trail of peeled rubber in his wake.

Maya took a deep breath and tried to calm herself, the top of her head resting against the door. Hands trembling, her eyes stung with the tears she refused to let fall.

How could he do this? It took every ounce of strength she had not to think of him constantly. Last night, when she saw his name on her cell phone caller ID, she nearly fell to pieces. The girls were snuggled in her bed as she read them a story, so she was forced to keep it together.

Today, she woke up determined to get over him. After all, the girls were back.

Shouldn't that be enough?

Why did he have to make a scene in front of her ex? He said the words she felt every moment since she stepped out of his door—that it was a mistake to walk away from what they shared.

How was she supposed to recover from that?

Maya stepped inside the apartment. Carlos sat on the sofa, still not dressed. His thick arms folded over his paunchy belly.

"You wanna tell me what that was about?"

"You wanna mind your own business?" She glared at him, then glanced at the flowers in her hand.

He remembered.

Amethyst calla lilies. Her favorite. Maya couldn't trash them. She grabbed a vase and headed to the kitchen.

Carlos was hard on her heels, though he didn't say anything. He leaned against the fridge and watched her.

"What?" She shrugged, then resumed snipping the stems of the lilies and placing them neatly in the vase.

Carlos raised a brow. "Are we really gonna play this game, Maya? I need to know who this man is. If he poses a threat to you or to my daughters."

"Because if he's interested in me he must be a psychopath, right?" She cut her eyes at him before returning her gaze to the task of arranging the flowers.

"That's not what I meant, and you know it. It's apparent you guys had something going on. That you're over it and he's not. Sounds like the guy could be a problem."

"He isn't a stalker, and he won't be a problem." She turned toward him. "He's an incredible guy. That's all you need to know."

"I didn't think this would be an issue any time soon, but I think maybe now is a good time for us to set some rules about you bringing men around my daughters." His gaze was defiant.

She wanted to hit the smug son of a bitch with the cast-iron skillet her mother gave her when she got married. Every woman should have a good cast iron skillet, *mi hija*, her mother had said. Only she hadn't specified exactly how the skillet should be used.

Maya slowly released a breath. This was her home. Her daughters were in the other room sleeping. She wouldn't have them wake up to their parents in a screaming match, especially when the topic was pointless. Not that Carlos needed to know that.

Just a few more hours and he'd be out of there. Back on a plane to return home to his precious wife. The woman who'd replaced her. She needed to relax. First, there was one more thing she needed to say.

"Don't you dare come in here and question my parenting skills. Everything I've done has been for the girls. I have always put them first, so I don't want to hear another word about Liam. Nor do I need dating advice from you."

Maya snatched the box of truffles off the kitchen counter and headed for her room. Grabbing her things, she headed for the bathroom. She stripped, turned on the shower and sat in the tub, allowing the water to rain down on her, where it muffled her cries.

She'd barely turned off the water when there was a light knock at the door.

"Mami, are you okay?"

Maya sighed. The girls' bedroom was next to the bathroom wall. They must've heard her crying. She pulled on her robe and cracked the door. Both girls stood there in their pajamas. Ella gripped her favorite teddy bear. Concern crimped their gorgeous little faces.

"I'm fine, baby," she said to Sofie, running a hand through her hair.

"Then why were you crying?" Ella asked, her eyes wide with concern.

"Mami's sad," Sofie told her little sister before Maya could answer.

"No, baby, you're wrong." Maya knelt in front of the girls. She kissed their foreheads and hugged them to her. "How could Mami ever be sad when she has you?"

Hugging her daughters made everything feel good and right. She needed to hold on to that feeling. To believe that what she said was true.

Chapter 22

It'd been nearly three weeks since Maya asked him not to contact her again.

He'd respected her wishes. Still, thoughts of her invaded his brain. Her laugh, her smile, her sarcastic sense of humor and the lilt of her unique accent. The way she made him feel. He'd peeled back his hardened layers and let her inside. They'd formed a deep connection. One he hadn't realized he'd been longing for.

Being with Maya gave him the same sort of adrenaline high he sought from BASE jumping or skydiving. His heart pounding like a drum, anticipating what came next. She obviously felt it, too. But not enough to ring him.

Liam tapped his fingers on his desk and sighed. Even if she had rung, where would they go from there? He'd never dated a woman with children. No matter how big the name on the marquee. It had been one of his hard-and-fast rules. Even knowing about Maya's two little girls, he couldn't shake his deep attachment to her. The feeling that his life would be better with her in it, even if that meant making room in it for her daughters.

"Liam." The sound of his assistant's voice coming from the phone's intercom roused him from his thoughts. "Mr. Johnston is here. He'd like to see you, if you can spare a moment."

"Of course. Give me a minute and send him in." Liam stretched his neck and shifted in his seat. Work. That's what he was supposed to be doing. Not daydreaming about Maya Can't-Be-Arsed-To-Ring-Him Alvarez.

"Liam, how are you?" The door swung open and Mitchell stepped inside his office wearing his usual broad smile. He shut the door behind him and took a seat in front of Liam's desk, not waiting to be asked. Liam liked that about him.

"I'm well. Hope you are, too." He took a sip of his cooled coffee.

"I am. Thanks for asking." There was an uneasy expression on Mitchell's face that made Liam straighten his spine, bracing himself for whatever he would say next. "I wanted to talk to you." He paused, weighing his next words carefully. "You seem a little distracted lately. Everything good, chief?"

Liam groaned. "That blatant, is it?"

Mitchell leaned forward in his chair. "Don't mean to pry, but there's an awful lot riding on this project for everyone involved. You insisted on running point. The team needs to know your head is in the game. We can't afford—"

"For me to muck up the entire affair?" Relief washed over Mitchell's face as he settled back into the chair. Liam held up a hand. "You're right. I've been distracted. I apologize."

Mitchell shifted in his seat. "No need to apologize. The team just needs to know our skipper is all-in."

"He will be." Liam tapped his finger on the desk and nodded toward Mitchell. "You will be."

Mitchell raised his hands in surrender. "I don't need to be the one in charge."

"You're the best man for the job. What I value most is your unwillingness to accept a piss-poor effort from any member of this team—including me. I'm grateful you spoke up. You'll do a smashing job. Anything you need, just let me know."

"Thanks for the vote of confidence, chief." Mitchell stood. He seemed to take a deep breath, then he sat down again. "I just wanted to say I know you're a long way from home—from family and friends. If you ever need to talk, I'm here."

Liam tried not to chuckle at the obvious discomfort the man felt. Mitchell was hired by the man he replaced, so he hadn't been keen on Liam when he first took over. Truthfully, he couldn't blame Mitchell. He'd come off as an ass back then, angry over being assigned to the project. Over the past months, they'd forged an understanding. He liked the chap. More every day. Perhaps they'd never be mates, but there wouldn't be any harm in grabbing a pint at the end of the day on occasion.

"Perhaps I'll take you up on the offer one day." Liam managed a grateful smile.

"Good. Because my sister-in-law is having a party this Labor Day weekend. You should join us. Alison's parties are always great. You'll have a good time."

"Thanks for the invite, but I'm not the best company lately."

"That's why you should come," Mitchell insisted. "The party is on Saturday. A few other guys from the office will be there. I'll email you the details. Just consider it."

Liam agreed, begrudgingly, and sent Mitchell on his way. Then he got down to work and finally stopped obsessing over the phone, mocking him with its silence.

Chapter 23

The last thing Maya wanted to do was attend a backyard barbecue. Kendra felt obliged to attend the annual Labor Day party Kai's aunt and uncle hosted. Still, she didn't want to go alone, so she shanghaied Maya and the girls.

Maya tried to muster enthusiasm for the party. After all, Alison and her husband, Marcus, were a nice enough couple. They always invited the girls to their sons' birthday parties.

She should be glad for some adult conversation while the girls played with their friends. But despite the brave face she put on for the girls, her heart ached for Liam. The distance between them only made the truth clearer. She'd fallen in love with him.

Rookie mistake.

How could she think a man like Liam would want to take on a woman with two children? Or that he could forgive her, when he couldn't forgive his own brother?

She shuddered, thinking of the day he'd showed up at

her door, proclaiming he wanted her. He wanted more of what they shared. Just the two of them with the freedom to do anything they pleased. That wasn't her reality. Her reality consisted of carting the girls off to school and to afterschool sports, cooking, cleaning, doing laundry, fielding arguments, bandaging bruised knees, and tucking them in at night with a story. She loved her life with the girls, but Liam didn't fit in to it.

Still, it meant the world that he'd been willing to try. He put his pride on the shelf and showed up at her door, flowers in hand. As tempting as his offer was, she wouldn't subject the girls to a rich man's experiment with domestic life. She had to do what was best for them.

"Ready!" Ella emerged from her room in a shirt, pants and pair of galoshes that made her look like an adorable little clown.

Maya smiled at her daughter. "Maybe we should think about a few tiny adjustments." She peeked through a small space between her thumb and forefinger.

Ella giggled. "Okay, Mami."

"I told you you looked like a disaster," Sofie, her little fashionista, moaned.

"*Disaster* is a very strong word," Maya said. "Let's just say the look is a little too adventurous for the occasion. No worries, we'll fix you up in no time."

Maya followed Ella to the bedroom she shared with her sister. She smiled as her daughter modeled outfits for the party. This was her life, and she loved being there for Sofie and Ella, helping to shape them into the women they would someday become. It was the most important job she could ever have.

Nothing else mattered.

Maya and the girls rode to the party with Kendra and Kai. He was invited to a friend's birthday party later on in the evening, so they planned to leave the party early. Alison wouldn't hear of it. She insisted that Maya and the girls stay, promising that someone would give them a ride home later. Maya hadn't been able to say no to the girls' sorrowful brown eyes.

She sat in the corner of the backyard, a glass of wine in hand. Kendra nudged her sister's shoulder.

"I know you don't want to talk about this anymore, but it's obvious how much you care for the guy."

Maya sipped her wine. "I'm not thinking about him."

Kendra raised an eyebrow. "Girl, please. I can practically see hearts where your irises should be, and you've got that lovesick look on your face. You've got it bad, and it's terminal."

Maya set her glass on a nearby table. "Even if I was, it doesn't matter. I'll get over it."

"Hate to state the obvious, but he knows about the girls, and he still wants to be with you. Maybe you should give him a chance."

"I can't risk introducing him into their lives, only to have him bolt when things get tough. Their father already abandoned them. The man who had a moral and biological obligation to be there for them."

"I know the prospect of bringing someone into your world feels scary, but don't make decisions based on fear. That's no way to live. Maybe you should give Liam a shot and trust that your daughters are the strong little women you've raised them to be."

Kendra became a blur as tears filled Maya's eyes. Panic filled her chest. She needed to get out of there before she made a fool of herself.

There's no crying at backyard barbecues. Pull it together.

"Marcus, honey, we're almost out of ice." Alison approached her husband. "That's why I asked you to pick up the large bags, not the small ones."

"We'll get more ice." Kendra stood and raised her hand. "Maya and I will. If you guys could just keep an eye on our kids until we get back."

"Oh thank God!" Alison blew out a breath in relief. "There are a few other things we need, too, if you wouldn't mind. I'll give you the money."

Maya wiped the tears from her face and forced a smile, grateful for her sister.

"You made it." Mitchell took a case of imported beer and three bottles of wine from Liam as he made his way into the kitchen. "Alison, this is my boss, Liam Westbrook."

"Pleased to meet you, Liam." Alison shook his hand. "You come bearing gifts. Thanks."

"The pleasure is mine," Liam said. "Thank you for having me."

"Please, make yourself at home. Mitchell, be sure to introduce Liam to everyone."

Great. There were few things he loathed more than being paraded around like a puppy dog. He preferred to get to know people organically, on his own terms.

"Mitchell, where are your beautiful wife and daughter?" he asked, hoping to delay the introduction parade.

"Folks I drink beer with call me Mitch." The man smiled as he grabbed a beer, then handed one to Liam. "Let's go find them."

Liam followed Mitch onto the back deck, where his wife, Monique, was seated with their little girl, Stella, on her lap. Monique was beautiful. Her warm brown skin glowed in the late-summer heat and her nearly coal-black hair fell to her bare shoulders. Stella had her mother's large expressive eyes and adorable nose. Her dark ringlets were pulled back with a frilly pink headband. Monique's arm—from which the little girl was trying to free herself, so she could join the bigger children—was covered in vibrant tattoos.

Mitchell had his hands full with these two, but he didn't pity the man. Instead, there was an unfamiliar twinge in his chest.

Envy.

Mitchell was content. The beaming smile he wore was present whenever he talked about his wife and daughter. The guy looked like he'd died and gone to heaven. He was head over heels about both of them.

Liam always considered guys like Mitch to be pathetic souls living on a cloud of delusion. Only now he wanted that contentment for himself. The way he felt when he was with Maya.

Monique stood and shook his hand firmly. A wide smile lit her face.

"Nice to finally meet you, Liam. Glad you could make it."

"Glad to be here." He'd been holed up in his penthouse, licking his wounds over a bottle of Scotch, since Maya walked out.

"Sorry to put you both on babysitting duty the minute you walk in the door, but this one needs her diaper changed. So if you don't want to do it…"

"No, by all means. Go." Mitch raised his hands in mock surrender. He leaned in and gave his wife a quick kiss, then planted another on his daughter's forehead. "We've got this. They're just little kids. How bad could it be?"

Monique crooked an eyebrow and shook her head. "Amateurs. You have no clue. They're a bunch of shifty little critters, especially that Roberts boy from down the street. Keep an eye on that one." She walked away, snickering.

Liam pulled out a chair and sat. "Would you think less of me if I admit I'm a teeny bit afraid of them?"

"She's just trying to scare us." Mitch took a swallow of his beer, then added under his breath, "I think."

"Well, that's reassuring." Liam took a sip of his own beer.

Within five minutes, a little girl shrieked. All of the children gathered around the spot on the ground where a little girl with dark wavy hair and tawny skin sat crying. Her knee was bleeding. Another girl, an older version of the first, poked a little boy in the chest.

"You hurt my sister!" the little girl screamed as she shoved the boy again.

Everything happened in a blur. Within seconds, Mitch and Liam were there. Mitch pulled apart the little girl and the little boy—who he'd bet anything was that Roberts boy. Liam knelt on the ground beside the little girl who was hurt.

"Hello there, beautiful." He offered a smile. "What seems to be the matter?"

She sniffled and her wailing turned into more of a moan. "It's…my…knee. He pushed me off the swing." She pointed an accusatory finger at the little boy.

"Is it okay if I take a look at your knee to make sure it's okay?"

She nodded tentatively, eyeing him warily. As he reached out to touch her leg, she howled. "But don't touch it!"

"If I don't touch it, how will I know it's okay?"

"Just look at it," she said.

Obviously. Why didn't I think of that? Liam was barely able to suppress a smile. *A woman who knows what she wants and isn't shy about telling you.*

"All right, then." He leaned in closer to examine her wound, while several of the other children stood over him, supervising the entire affair.

"The skin is scraped, and it's bleeding a little. You'll be fine, love. We need to clean the cut, though."

"No!" She pulled her leg back, then winced in pain. She started to cry again.

The older girl knelt beside her and put an arm around her shoulder. "Don't cry, Ella. He needs to clean the cut, just like Mommy does when you get a boo-boo, okay?"

"But it always hurts," Ella cried. "I want Mommy. Where's Mommy?"

The older girl surveyed the backyard. "Mommy and *tia* are still at the store. She'll be back soon. Just don't cry anymore. I'll hold your hand. It'll be okay. Promise."

"Ella, is it?" Liam looked to the older girl for confirmation. She nodded. "You have a pretty special big sister to take care of you. You're a lucky girl," Liam said. "What's your sister's name?"

"Sofia, but we call her Sofie."

"Okay, Ella. I'm going to find something to clean that knee up. Sofie will stay right here and hold your hand while I clean your boo-boo. Is that okay?" Ella leaned into her sister, her head buried in the girl's shoulder, and nodded.

"Here's the first aid kit." Alison rushed over. The woman struck him as someone who was prepared for anything. She probably had an underground bunker stocked with two years' worth of canned food. "You want me to take care of it?"

"No, I can handle it. Thanks." Liam took the box and rummaged through it. He found antiseptic wipes, some ointment and bandages. "Okay, Ella. Here we go. We're going to make your knee all better, love."

Liam carefully cleaned the cut. The girl whimpered a little, but held relatively still so he could clean her scrape, apply the ointment and then bandage it. He balled up the waste and put it in Alison's outstretched hand. "All better. Can you stand up for me?"

Liam offered Ella a hand, but as he tried to pull her to her feet, she whimpered in pain again. "It hurts."

"It's okay, love. Nothing's broken, but it will probably sting for a few more minutes. Shall I pick you up?"

Ella nodded and held her arms up to him. The need to help and protect this little person who couldn't fend for herself was strange and unsettling. He wondered about his own nephew, whom he'd never seen in person. A twinge of guilt gnawed at his gut as he climbed to his feet, then lifted the girl into his arms. She immediately buried her little face in his shoulder and wrapped her arms around his neck. A gesture that was as comforting to him as it must have been for her.

He always thought of kids as takers. Always in need of something. Feeding. Burping. Their nappies changed. Maybe he could understand the sense of purpose parents derived from having a little person rely on them. Liam patted the girl's back.

"Not to worry. Everything will be fine. We'll find your mum, as soon as she returns."

She nodded, her voice muffled. "'Kay. I'll stay with you."

Ella sat on Liam's lap as he sat at the table with Mitch, Monique and Stella. Sofie stayed at her sister's side for the first five minutes, then she migrated back to the play area with the other children. Thirty minutes later, Sofie yelled in their direction, "Mommy and Tia Kendra are here!"

Ella raised her head, looking in the general direction in which her sister pointed.

"Would you like to show your mommy what happened to your knee, and how it's all better now?" Liam asked. The little girl's eyes brightened and she nodded, but she made no move to get down from his lap. "Shall I walk you over?"

She shook her head. "My leg still hurts."

"Right, then." He smiled. "I'll take you to her. Show me the way."

Liam carried Ella to the other side of the backyard where two women stood. The taller woman, who had short curly black hair and smooth dark brown skin watched as he approached. Her eyes grew wide as saucers. She tapped the other woman—whose back was to him—more frantically the closer he got.

"What is it, Kendra?" the woman said, in an all-too-familiar voice as she whipped around. Her eyes widened and she covered her open mouth.

Liam froze in his tracks, her name caught in his throat as their eyes met. *It couldn't be.* "Maya? What are you doing…"

Liam looked at Ella's little face, then at Maya's again. *Of course.* Ella was Maya's daughter. Same chocolate-brown hair, but with a looser wave, where Maya's had a more defined curl. Same precocious eyes and pouty mouth. They even had the same button nose. Ella's tawny skin was closer to the color of Maya's ex's.

She stepped forward and took her daughter from his arms, hitching the girl on one hip. Her feet dangled to Maya's knees. "Ella, what happened to your knee?"

"Billy pushed me off the swing." She pointed in the direction of the Roberts boy.

"Sweetie, I'm so sorry I wasn't here." Maya kissed the girl's forehead and tucked her head beneath her chin as she rubbed her back. "Who bandaged your knee?"

"Mr. Lee?" Ella said, inflection in her voice.

Maya looked up at Liam, as if just realizing again that he was there. "Mr. Liam? Well, that was very nice of him. Did you thank him?"

The girl nodded, then said, "Thank you, Mr. Liam."

Liam stuffed his hands in the pockets of his trousers and smiled. "My pleasure, Ella. Hope your knee feels better now."

"A little," she said.

"Enough for Tia Kendra to take you inside and get you an ice cream?" Maya's friend asked.

The little girl bolted upright, nearly headbutting her

mother as she wriggled toward the ground. Maya let Ella down so she could grab the other woman's outstretched hand.

"Thanks, Kendra." Maya nodded toward the woman who looked enough like her to be her sister or at least a cousin.

Kendra gave them both a knowing smile then led the little girl away.

The moments that passed before Maya finally turned and looked at him felt torturous. She cleared her throat and crossed her arms, bare in a white sleeveless top. "Thank you for taking care of Ella's knee."

Maya could barely force the words from her throat or raise her eyes to his. This had to be a crazy dream. Liam freaking Westbrook was standing in the backyard of a family friend. Every handsome inch of him.

"Maya." Liam stepped forward and placed a gentle hand on her arm. She trembled at his touch and the way he whispered her name as he had so many nights when she lay in his arms. "I've missed you."

Maya's heart squeezed in her chest and tears stung her eyes. She wished there was a way to make her obligations as a mother and her feelings for Liam work. There was no viable solution. His presence now didn't change that.

She finally raised her eyes to his. "Liam, what are you doing here? How'd you end up with my daughter?"

He pointed toward the table where Mitch and Monique watched them with great interest. "Mitch and I work together. He felt sorry for me, I suppose. I've been moping about like a pathetic arse who hasn't a friend in the world."

The pain in her chest inched up a notch. Breathing was more difficult. She lowered her gaze, no longer able to hold his.

Liam loosely gripped her other arm. "Maya, please. Look at me."

She heaved a sigh, her hands shaking as she dragged her gaze back to his. The warmth of his hands and the heat of his impassioned gaze threatened to raise her body temperature to a fever pitch. He was her personal kryptonite, breaking down every one of her defenses with his steely gaze.

She gasped, her body vibrating with the sensations stirred by his touch.

"My darling Maya." He trailed a hand up her arm and shoulder and grazed her cheek with his thumb. "I can hardly believe it's you."

Maya stepped away, glancing toward Mitch and Monique. "Not here," she whispered. "My daughters are here."

She headed across the backyard, and Liam fell in step beside her. They exited through a gate that led to a secluded space between the houses.

Maya leaned against the fence, her chest heaving as if she'd run a marathon. Before she could speak, he pressed his mouth to hers. His familiar weight pinned her against the hard white vinyl fence. Her resistance fell away as her mouth surrendered to the heat of his and the longing that filled her body. Maya pressed her fingers into his back, pulling him closer as she angled her head to taste more of him.

For a moment, she didn't care where she was, or who was watching. The distant approach of an ice-cream truck brought her out of her daze where only the two of them existed. Maya wedged her hands between them, creating space. She blinked back the tears that made Liam a blur.

"Liam, I'm sorry. I can't."

"Maya, I want you in my life. Every day. Nothing has been the same since you walked out. I nearly blew a major deal at work because I can't get you out of my head, no matter how hard I try."

"What are you saying?" She bit her lower lip. Her eyes searched his.

"You consume my every thought." He grazed her cheek with his thumb. "All I can think of is the warmth of your smile. The sound of your laugh. The way you taste. I should have fought for you. For us."

"But you didn't." Her voice was shaky. Her gaze met his. There was more than just sadness there. There was hurt and anger.

He had no excuse to offer. "I should have told you how I felt. That I was—"

Maya placed her fingers to his mouth. "Don't say something you don't mean. I couldn't bear that." He wanted to object, but her eyes pleaded with him to let her finish. "Our summer together was remarkable. Let's not ruin it by forcing this to be something it isn't. Or pretending to be who we aren't."

Liam pressed his forehead to hers and gripped her shoulders. He needed to find the right words. To make her believe him. He'd been a world-class bullshitter his entire life. It'd always worked for him, but Maya was unlike anyone he'd known. He wanted to be straight with her. Even if that meant revealing his soul, stripped down and bare, giving her a glimpse of his raw, bleeding heart.

He trusted her with it.

It was time to throw out the bullshit and be sincere, turn off his brain and tell her how he felt. He took her hand and placed it over his heart. "I know what I said…what I wanted in the beginning. You changed all of that for me. You're all I want."

She shrugged, her features pinched. "You can't have just me. I'm a package deal."

He smiled faintly. "I noticed. Sofie and Ella are beautiful. I can't believe I didn't recognize them right away. They look so much like you. They even inherited your fiery spirit."

"You have no idea." A faint smile kissed her lips.

His jaw clenched and he shoved his hands in his pockets. "Not knowing the girls...that wasn't my choice."

"They were away for the summer with their father and I just..." She sighed, a crimson glow beneath her warm brown skin. "It felt good to just be me for a little while. Not a mother, or a wife. Just Maya. For two beautiful months you gave that to me. But it's time for me to go back to my real life. Sofia and Gabriella are my life. I'm their mother every day. Weekends, too. That means I have to make hard grown-up choices. Do what's best for them, even if it's the opposite of what I want for myself. I know you don't understand that because your life is about what you want..."

"What's that supposed to mean?"

"You put your ego ahead of your relationship with your family and the best interest of the company your father worked his entire life to build for you. If you can't sacrifice your pride enough to mend the fences with your own family, how can I expect you to do that for mine?"

Damn. A fierce body blow delivered straight to the gut.

He winced. The feeling was so visceral, he was surprised that he wasn't on his knees coughing up blood. It was painfully clear why she felt she couldn't trust him to be in their lives.

He'd been selfish most of his life, particularly since his mother's death. However, over the past months, he'd slowly developed a need to care for Maya. To put her interests ahead of his. An unfamiliar feeling fluttered in his chest.

His face must've reflected the pain of the devastating blow she landed, because her countenance softened and she squeezed his arm.

"I'm sorry. I didn't mean to sound so harsh." He diverted his gaze from hers. Hurt and anger welled in his chest. The latter was directed at himself because she was right. Still, he didn't respond, so she continued. "I'm not saying you're a selfish person. Just that your life revolves around what you want. There's nothing wrong with that. But my life is the complete opposite. Please say you understand."

"That you believe I haven't a selfless bone in my body?" He crooked an eyebrow, and did his level best to strain the hurt and anger from his voice. "Loud and clear. I should be insulted by your remark. Instead, I'm overwhelmed by the need to prove to you it isn't true."

"Liam—"

"I know that's who I've been. That isn't who I want to be anymore. I need you in my life. As for the girls, I've known them for an hour and already I'm smitten with them. How could I not care for them?" He brushed the hair from her eyes. "They're part of you."

She pressed her back into the fence, seemingly desperate to create space between them. Her voice was laced with sadness. "People don't change overnight, Liam." She locked eyes with him. "Walking away is the best option for both of us."

"I know you, Maya. This isn't what you want." He gripped her shoulders. The muscles tensed beneath his fingertips. Regardless of what she said, her feelings were written all over her face. Pain. Passion. Desire. Perhaps, even love. She was terrified by all of it, but she wanted it, wanted him. He needed to make her see it.

"You think you know me, that you want to be with me. But the person you know I'd almost forgotten. Because that's not who I have to be for my daughters. I'm the woman who referees arguments about which Saturday-morning cartoons my girls will watch. Who has to decide between sending my daughters to private school or being able to afford an apartment in a better neighborhood."

"Maybe I don't know everything about you, but that wasn't my choice."

"True, but if I hadn't kept it from you, we wouldn't be

here now, because you wouldn't have given a single mother a second glance."

His cheeks burned. What could he say in defense of himself? She was right.

She sighed. "I'm not judging you for that or making excuses for what I've done. I just need you to understand why we have to follow the script." Her countenance softened. She pressed a hand to his cheek. "Today was an inconvenient surprise. One I doubt will happen again. I don't regret our time together, but I can't offer anything more. Our decision was a good one. Let's stay the course."

Maya gave him a quick peck on the cheek, but he pulled her into his arms and pressed his mouth to hers. She froze, not responding, not pushing him away. Then her body softened, relaxing into him, her mouth opening to his.

Liam held her in his arms. Poured everything they had been, every moment they'd shared, into that one kiss. He kissed her, as if it would be their last, hoping with every beat of his wounded, bleeding heart that it wouldn't.

She was wrong. He did know her, and he'd do whatever it took to prove it to her.

Finally, she pulled her mouth from his as she pressed her hands into his chest. "This isn't just about you and me. I have to do what's best for my daughters. I can't bring you into their lives knowing one day you'll disappear and break their hearts."

"Is it their hearts you're worried about or your own?" He said the words gently, but she bristled at them, just the same.

"Both." The sincerity of that one word made him want to promise her the world. That he'd never hurt her. But he wouldn't make a promise he couldn't keep. Relationships were messy and people got hurt. Not every relationship was meant to be forever, regardless of how much both people might want it. They'd never find out unless they gave it an honest go.

It can't be over.

Not when they both wanted this so badly. He only needed the chance to prove he could be the man she needed. That the girls needed. He tightened his jaw and tried to hold back the emotion that made his chest ache.

"Please." His grip on her hand tightened. "You and I, we've both been through a lot. For the first time in a long time we found someone who makes us truly happy. That can't have been for nothing. Don't you see? Meeting the night of your birthday, seeing each other today…that can't all be a meaningless coincidence."

She worried her lower lip, tears rolling down her cheeks. "What are you saying? This is fate?"

"I'm saying there's only one way to find out. We must be brave enough to try." He wiped the tears from her cheek with his thumb.

Maya sniffled. She smiled and extended her open palm to him. "Hi, I'm Maya Alvarez. I'm the divorced mother of two little girls, Sofia and Gabriella. I'm not glamorous or spectacular, but I do enjoy an exciting adventure every now and again."

He grinned, the tension in his body releasing as he took her hand in his and shook it. "I'm Liam Westbrook. My family builds luxury resorts all over the world. I've spent way too much of my time chasing the glamorous life and extreme sports. Suddenly, none of that seems important. I have zero experience with children, but I don't bite, at least not usually, and I'm already housebroken. I think I just might be a perfect fit for a family of three bossy women, if they'll give me a chance."

Maya was still smiling as tears flowed down her cheeks. She nodded. "Okay, maybe we could start with you giving us a lift home."

Chapter 24

He'd wiped Maya's tears, stolen another kiss and then agreed to her terms. They would take things slowly, so as not to upset the girls. That meant returning to the party as if nothing had happened. Not an easy thing to do with nearly every adult set of eyeballs on them as they reentered the gate.

Still, he managed to enjoy the party, despite watching Maya from a distance. It was nice spending the day with down-to-earth people on a hot afternoon. Far different from the upscale events he often frequented where the paparazzi camped out to get photos of celebrities and socialites. Today was relaxed and unpretentious. A breath of fresh air.

The appeal of suburban neighborhoods like this one became clear. There was a sense of community and family he didn't experience with high-rise living. Or even in his flat back in London.

Liam watched the families interacting around the fire pit. He'd always pitied couples with children, pushing their prams down the street or corralling children at the play area in the mall. Maybe all this time, it was they who pitied him. A man who was completely alone in the moments that truly mattered.

Maya approached him with a shy smile that reminded him of the first night they met. "I told Mitch and Monique you were kind enough to offer us a ride home."

"Ready to go, then?"

"Yes. I just need to round up the girls." She scanned the backyard. Her gaze landed on the spot on the deck where the girls were playing some kind of board game with Alison's boys. She walked toward them. "Sofia, Gabriella, time to go. Get your things."

"But why, Mami? We don't have school tomorrow." Ella's adorable little voice made him feel sorry for her.

"I know, but you still need your rest, so it's time to go. No more lip." She planted a kiss on the girl's forehead and tapped her lightly on the bottom.

"Okay." When Maya walked away, Ella sighed. "It didn't work."

Liam laughed. "You've got a little con artist on your hands."

Maya laughed, too. "That one keeps me on my toes, but she's a sweet kid. She just needs boundaries."

"They're both gorgeous and clever like their mum."

"Thank you." She faced him, her smile giving way to a more serious expression. "I really am sorry I didn't tell you about them from the beginning."

"I've learned not to trust many people. So it hurt that you hadn't been completely honest with me. I understand why you felt you couldn't be. So I'm sorry, too."

"Why?"

"For being the kind of shallow pillock who wouldn't have seen beyond you being the mum of two small girls.

You saved me from what might have been the biggest mistake of my life."

Maya's eyes were shiny, the orange glow of the fire reflected in them. "Liam, I—"

"Is Mr. Liam going with us?" Ella and her sister approached wearing colorful kid-sized backpacks.

"Yes, he's giving us a ride home." Maya reached down to zip Ella's Dora the Explorer backpack, its contents threatening to spill out.

Liam squatted so his eyes were level with little Ella's. "Is that all right with you?"

A wide smile spread across her face. She nodded and wrapped her little arms around his neck, nearly knocking him off balance. He laughed and patted her on the back.

"Well, that's settled, then."

The ride to Maya's apartment was filled with the girls' chatter in the backseat and their rapid-fire questions for him. Maya interfered when she felt they were being too nosy or when their minor sibling arguments became too heated.

She was amazing with the girls. She knew just what to say to satisfy their curiosity without divulging too much information. She was warm and loving, but firm when she needed to be. His mum would've liked her very much. And she would have adored the girls.

He parked in front of their building and turned the car off. "Here we are. Safe and sound, as promised."

He was glad they'd taken this step forward. Still, there was so much he needed to say. With the girls hanging on every word, they hadn't been able to talk on the short ride to her flat. "Would it be okay if I came in for a bit?"

Maya was interrupted by the cheers of the girls. "Yay, Mr. Liam is coming to our house. Mr. Liam, I want to show you my Barbies, 'kay?"

Liam's gaze settled on Ella's big brown eyes, reflected in the rearview mirror. He couldn't imagine disappointing that little face, radiant as a beam of sunshine at midday. He shifted his gaze to Maya. "If it's all right with your mummy."

She seemed relieved at their request. "Okay, but only for a little while. Then you two are taking your baths and going to bed. Agreed?"

"We promise, Mami."

He exited the car, then opened the doors for Maya and the girls.

Ella grabbed his hand and tugged. "C'mon, Mr. Liam. We'll show you our apartment and our bedroom. I share with Sofie."

"Stop being so bossy, *Mami.*" Maya dug in her purse, producing her keys.

"Yes, Mami." Ella lowered her long eyelashes. Her tone was reserved and conciliatory as she tugged on Liam's hand. This one was an adorable handful, and he was in serious danger of turning into putty in her little hands.

Maya seemed nervous as she opened the door to her flat. He followed her inside, taking in the cozy space. It was neat, decorated with eclectic furniture that was tasteful, yet showed Maya's unique sense of style. The walls were neutral, yet the space was filled with deep, rich colors provided by the furnishings and art.

The girls returned with their Barbie dolls and a host of accessories, including a swanky beach house. He sat cross-legged on the floor driving Barbie and her little friends around in a small radio-controlled dune buggy as the girls squealed and chased the car. Later, Sofie enlisted his help with a puzzle that featured a red-haired mermaid and a crab.

Maya sipped café con leche as she looked on in near silence. After nearly an hour, she announced it was time for the girls to get ready for bed. He whined in objection nearly as much as the girls did until Maya gave them all a look that indicated the case was closed.

She squeezed his arm, promising to return once the girls were tucked in to bed.

Liam surveyed the photos and mementos on display on the fireplace mantle and tables. Pictures of the girls at various stages. Pictures of a couple who had to be her parents. Photos of her sister, Kendra, and her son. A jar filled with sand and seashells. A frame made of wooden craft sticks, painted in bright colors by a child's hand, held a lovely photo of Maya and the girls.

He smiled. They were a lovely trio. How could Carlos just walk away from them?

Suddenly, Maya stood beside him. "The girls want to say good-night."

He followed her down the hall to their bedroom, painted in a bubblegum pink. The twin beds, dressers and nightstand were white. Posters of cartoon characters adorned the walls. The light was a miniature chandelier. Perfect for two little princesses.

"Hey there, girls." Liam stepped inside the room. A warmth he couldn't explain filled his chest. "Off to bed now?"

"Yes," they said in unison.

"Would you read us a story?" Sofie held up a book nearly as big as she.

"Sofie, that is *not* what we agreed to." Maya took the book from her daughter's hand. "You two are in rare form tonight."

"I don't mind," Liam said. "If you don't."

"Fine, but I'll pick the book." Maya shoved the large book on a bookshelf, then surveyed the lot of them, producing a small, square book with just a few thick cardboard pages. She handed the book to Liam. "He'll read this one instead."

Maya moved a small chair from the corner and placed it between the girls' beds, then gestured for Liam to sit down.

He sat in the tiny chair, his knees nearly poking him in the chin. The girls fell into a fit of giggles. Maya laughed, too. He couldn't blame them. Must have been quite a sight. Besides, forcing his large frame into a chair meant for Thumbelina was a small price to pay to hear Maya's joyous laughter once again.

"Ready, then?" The girls nodded enthusiastically, and he began to read the story of the little mouse who set out on an adventure.

Liam hadn't read a children's book in ages. But sitting there with Maya and her girls felt like the thing in his life he hadn't realized was missing.

Maya sat quietly in a rocking chair in the corner as he read. She'd been watching him with the girls from the moment he stood in that backyard with Ella in his arms, looking for evidence to prove that Liam wasn't father material.

But he'd been such a good sport. Patient. Sweet. Kind. He'd even worn the princess tiara Sofie insisted he wear to play Barbies with them.

A joy settled deep in her chest. Liam continued to surprise her. Everything about him was unexpected. She'd been terrified he would balk at the prospect of taking on two bossy little girls. Instead, he was a natural with them. Her heart squeezed in her chest as she watched the adoration on their little faces as he read the story, giving life to each character's unique voice. Something their own father could never be bothered to do.

Her babies were happy. And Liam seemed genuinely happy, as well.

She'd fallen a little more in love with Liam. Now it seemed Sofie and Ella were doing the same.

Liam finished reading the story, and despite the girls'

chorus of whining, she put her foot down. Lights out, the girls tucked in to bed, Liam trailed her down the narrow hallway back to the cramped living room. For the first time, she considered what he must think of her place. The entire apartment was smaller than the great room at his penthouse. Yet, here he was, in her living room, gazing at her like he was about to burst with a desire to touch her.

He stepped closer, his hands shoved into his pockets as if he needed to keep them restrained. "There's so much I'd like to say."

Maya gestured for him to sit down. She joined him on the couch, leaving as much space between them as she had the first day she laid eyes on him in that restaurant.

Liam slid his hand across the empty space between them and threaded his fingers through hers. The warmth from his hand flowed through her fingertips and sent her pulse racing. Heat crawled over her skin and lodged in her chest.

"Maya, I want to be with you and the girls. I know you were worried I wouldn't be good with them. To be honest, I wasn't sure how well I'd do either. They're amazing, like their mum. I've enjoyed every minute I spent with them today."

Her heart jumped in her chest. She bit her lip, trying to restrain the sense of joy and hope she felt. *Good* was an understatement. He'd been an absolute rock star with the girls. Caring for Ella's scraped knee. Patiently answering their questions on the ride home. Entertaining them by playing Barbies. Reading to them. The girls adored him. They'd taken to him so well. Both were pleasant surprises that filled her heart, nearly bringing her to tears.

Still, she had to be sure. Sofie's and Ella's happiness was at stake. "Today was one of those days when I can't believe how lucky I am to have them. But some days are filled with tantrums and tears. Theirs and mine. Will you still find our lives so fascinating then? Think about it, Liam, and answer honestly. I'll understand either way."

Liam studied her face for a moment, then let out a long sigh that made her stomach flip. "When I said I cared for you, I wasn't being honest, most of all with myself. I'm way beyond caring for you, Maya. I love you. And what I want more than anything is to be a part of your lives."

He loved her. Wanted her. All of her. The passionate lover and the dedicated mother. He was a complete blur as tears rolled down her cheeks.

"Saying goodbye to you was one of the hardest things I've ever done. So, please, don't get my hopes up unless you mean it."

Liam slid closer to her on the couch and took her face into his hands. He stared deep into her eyes as if he wanted her to see his very soul.

"Every word. I love you, Maya."

He leaned in, his warm breath skittering across her skin like butterfly wings. Liam pressed his mouth to hers, then peppered soft kisses on her wet cheeks before returning to her mouth. Her pulse raced. Every kiss felt like an unspoken promise. To love her. To be there for her and the girls.

Liam wrapped his arms around her, pulling her in closer. He kissed her with a sweet desperation that warmed her heart and intensified the heat between her thighs.

Maya let out a contented moan as his tongue slipped into her mouth. As his hands slid lower, gripping her bottom. Her internal temperature rose with each kiss. Each touch.

Liam broke their kiss. His dark eyes surveyed hers. "I don't expect you to say it now. But do you think you could ever—"

"Yes, I love you. So much."

His nervous laugh seemed to relieve both their tension. He pulled her in for another slow, sweet, torturous kiss as his hands glided down her back, then gently tugged at her blouse, pulling it from her waistband.

She missed this. Missed him. But it wasn't that simple. She wedged her hands between them, creating space and giving herself a moment to regain her clarity. Her body instantly ached for the heat of his. "We can't. The girls are here." She peeked around him and down the hall.

"They're asleep. Remember?" he mumbled between kisses planted on her neck and throat.

"They're also excited about you being here. One of them is bound to come looking for a glass of water or just being plain nosy." Maya sighed. "That's what I mean, I'm their mother first and always."

Liam gently kissed the palm of her hand. The simple gesture sent a wave of electricity through her body. A slight whimper escaped her mouth before she could restrain it. He smirked and kissed her wrist, then planted delicate kisses along her arm until he reached her elbow.

"You're not making it easy for me to hold on to my resolve here."

He looked up at her and grinned. "Where's the fun in that?"

She grinned. "Smart-ass."

"True. But you love this smart-ass." He kissed her again.

"I have a confession to make."

He studied her face. "Whatever it is, you can tell me."

"I'm terrified this won't work because we're so different. That one day you'll realize you'd prefer to be with someone more like you. Someone like Carlotta Mayfair."

He gave her a warm grin that eased her fears.

"Darling, you don't ever have to worry about me wanting Carlotta Mayfair or anyone else. None of them made me truly happy. Only you have that power. With you, I'm a better person. I know we're different, but don't you see, love? That's what makes us so right together. We balance each other like two halves coming together to make a whole. I believe that with all of my heart."

She smiled, tears clouding her vision. "Me, too."

"Good," he whispered, as he pulled her closer.

Maya leaned in to kiss him.

"Ooh… Mami's kissing Mr. Liam." Ella stood in the hallway, clutching a stuffed animal as she pointed at them.

Maya gave Liam an apologetic smile. She crossed the room to stand in front of her daughter, her hands on her hips. "What are you doing up? It's way past your bedtime."

"I'm not sleepy yet." Ella punctuated the statement with a yawn, then added, "And I'm thirsty. And you forgot to leave the night-light on and Sofie's scared." Ella sniffed, then scratched her leg.

"Sofie's scared, huh? Well, let's get you a very tiny glass of water. Then we'll turn on the night-light for your sister, so you can go back to bed and stay there. *¿Entiendes?*"

Ella nodded. She followed Maya in the direction of the kitchen before diverting her path and sitting next to Liam on the couch. "I saw you kissing Mami."

"Yes, well, there's certainly no denying that, is there?" He wiped lipstick from his mouth.

"Mami says a mommy and daddy kiss because they love each other. Do you love Mami?"

Liam smiled at Maya, standing over them, arms crossed. "I do. Very much, Ella."

The little girl grinned. "Then kiss her again."

"No, honey." Maya's eyes pinned Liam, ready to spring from the couch, in place.

"Don't you want to kiss him?" Ella's question was matter-of-fact.

"That isn't the point, sweetie."

"Do you want to kiss Mami?" Ella looked up at Liam, her eyes wide.

He smiled at Ella, then turned his gaze toward Maya.

"Very much. But your mum doesn't believe that's appropriate behavior, and I respect that."

"She just doesn't want me to see you kissing," Ella whispered loudly to Liam from behind her hand.

He chuckled. "Perceptive girl you've got here." He nodded toward the precocious little girl. "Not much you can put past this one."

Maya rolled her eyes and shook her head. "Tell me about it."

Ella turned to her mother. "If I go to bed, will you kiss him?"

Her little con artist was the master of the deal. Maya stifled the urge to laugh.

"Yes," Liam interjected. A wide smile spread across his handsome face. "But only if you hurry off to bed this instant."

Ella grabbed her teddy bear and hopped off the couch, but then she turned back, her lovely little face pinched in a thoughtful expression "Does this mean you're my daddy now?"

A curious mix of joy and sadness tinged her daughter's voice. Maya's heart broke. Ella wanted her to be happy. The girls had asked more than once why she hadn't gotten married again like their father had. Ella was clearly worried that her newfound affection for Liam meant she was in some way betraying her father. After Carlos's meeting with Liam, no doubt he'd planted the thought in Ella's little head.

Before Maya could respond, Liam draped his arm around the girl's shoulder. "You already have a daddy who loves you very much, Ella. I could never take his place. But I can be your friend, and I can care just as much for you, your sister and your mum as any daddy would. I'll also be there to box the ears of any mean little boy who pushes you off the swing. Would that be all right?"

Ella wrapped her wiry arms around Liam's neck and squeezed. She pressed a sloppy kiss to his cheek, then scampered toward the room she shared with her sister. She called over her shoulder, "I'm going to bed. You can kiss now."

Liam laughed as he wiped his cheek. He rose to his feet and took Maya in his arms. "Guess that's a yes."

"You don't have to do this," she whispered, then projected her voice in the direction of the hall. "I know Ella thinks she's the boss around here, but she isn't. I am."

He leaned in and pressed his mouth to hers, his fingers threading the hair at the nape of her neck as he pulled her into the kiss. A kiss sweet and warm, filled with deep affection. He smiled. "I'm a man of my word."

So he was.

And he was here. Where she wanted him. She was happy. Her world complete. She was with the man she loved. A man who loved and accepted every facet of her. Who didn't fear diving into her complicated life.

It was too soon to say whether this would last forever. But she felt safe. Loved. As she stared into Liam's eyes, she got the sense he felt the same.

And she couldn't be happier.

Epilogue

"Stop fidgeting. You look beautiful, and so do the girls." Liam removed his left hand from the steering wheel and squeezed Maya's hand. "Besides, we're only meeting my family, not the queen."

"I want to make a good impression. Is it so wrong that I want your family to like me?"

"Not at all." He made a left turn. The sun reflected off patches of ice peeking through the packed snow covering the road. "But it doesn't matter what my family thinks. I love you and the girls more than anything in the world. Nothing will change that."

Maya took a deep breath and smiled. "Thanks. I think I'm ready now."

"Good." He turned in to the long drive. The white, red and green Christmas lights strung overhead formed a tunnel leading to their family estate. "Because we're here."

Maya looked up and gasped. The house was impressive, he had to admit, especially decked out in its Christmas finery. Though not as lovely as it was when his mum had been alive to oversee the place. She'd done much of the gardening herself. The woman had loved her prized flower beds and the heated greenhouse, which allowed her to continue gardening in winter. She'd grown many of the fresh vegetables used in their kitchen. Emma Westbrook had firmly believed that working with the hands was good for the mind, body and soul.

Liam parked the car, then went round to open Maya's door.

Maya straightened her skirt again as soon as she emerged from the vehicle. "This is where you grew up? It's beautiful."

"It is." He opened the back passenger door and escorted the girls out.

"You lived here when you were little, like me?" Ella asked, her warm breath creating a cloud in the chilly air.

"Even younger. I was born in this house. Right in that room upstairs there." He pointed toward the second-floor master suite.

"Not at a hospital?" Sofie's chestnut-brown eyes widened. "That must have been a really long time ago. Like before they had hospitals."

Maya and Liam laughed.

"Way to make a fellow feel old, Sofie." He shoved her shoulder playfully. "There were indeed hospitals when I was born. I was impatient, even then. I refused to wait until my mum could make it to the hospital. A midwife delivered me here."

"Wow," the girls echoed.

Liam turned his attention to their mother, who was fiddling with the barrette in Sofie's hair. It'd been a little more than six months since he'd first laid eyes on her, and he could swear she got more beautiful every day. He swept her hair, worn in loose curls, to one side and planted a kiss on the side of her neck. "Relax, darling. They're going to love you."

A familiar voice called across the yard. "I'm freezing me buns off out here, child. Coming in any time soon?"

Liam broke into a wide grin. Mrs. Hanson was perhaps the only person in this family less patient than he.

He squeezed Maya's hand, and they headed toward the house. "C'mon, girls. There's someone I want you to meet." He released Maya's hand and succumbed to Mrs. Hanson's bear hug. For such a tiny thing, the woman had the arm strength of a black bear. "Good to see you, Mrs. Hanson."

"And you, my boy. I'm so pleased you brought your gorgeous girls along this time."

"Mrs. Hanson, this is Maya Alvarez."

Maya stepped forward, beaming, her hand extended. "It's a pleasure to finally meet you, Mrs. Hanson." The woman ignored her hand and hugged Maya as if she'd known her all her life. Maya relaxed into the woman's hug almost immediately.

"Thank you for the warm welcome." Maya smiled sheepishly. "Liam talks about you all the time. I feel like I already know you."

"And I you." Her eyes met Liam's and she gave him a wide smile.

Warmth filled his chest. Mrs. Hanson's smile was filled with love and approval. He gave her a small nod, acknowledging it.

"You've made quite an impression on this one." Mrs. Hanson jerked a thumb in Liam's direction. "He's been blathering on like a schoolboy about you." The older woman took a step back and surveyed Maya's warm brown skin. "Look at you! Even prettier than your pictures."

Maya thanked Mrs. Hanson. Her shoulders relaxed.

Mrs. Hanson leaned down so she was nearly at eye level with the girls. "And who are these two gorgeous little princesses? Wait, don't tell me. You must be Sofia. And you, little one, must be Gabriella."

"How'd you know our names?" Sofie asked.

"Because Liam talks about you two all the time. He's quite smitten, he is. Never thought I'd see the day when three women would have my boy wrapped around their little fingers. And him loving it, no less. There is a Savior in the heavens above, indeed." She laughed as she collected their coats. "C'mon in. Everyone's waiting to meet you girls."

"Well, that makes me feel special." Liam frowned. "Do you mean not a one of you is eager to see me?"

"I am." Hunter stood inside the entryway. "Good to see you, little brother."

Liam stepped inside and shook his brother's extended hand, then patted his shoulder. "You, too. How have you and the family been since my last visit?"

"Quite well, thank you. Merrie and the children are in the parlor with Father, awaiting your arrival."

Liam introduced Maya and the girls to his brother, then led them toward the parlor. He leaned down and whispered in Maya's ear, "You're quite the hit. Just take a deep breath, all right?"

She nodded and squeezed his hand. Her breathing calmed a bit, and she lifted her chin as they entered the warm, bright space off the back garden.

Merrie sat on the couch holding little Emma on her lap. The little girl had her mother's haunting gray eyes. She was a convivial little thing, full of personality. Much like his own mother, after whom the girl was named.

She grinned, raised her arms and wiggled her chubby fingers as Liam approached.

"Hello, Em. Don't you look beautiful today?" He lifted the girl from her mother's arms and rubbed his nose against hers. She giggled. He pressed a reassuring hand to Maya's lower back. "Merrie, this is Maya Alvarez and her daughters Sofia and Gabriella. Girls, this is Hunter's wife, Meredith, and my niece, Emma."

Merrie stood, taking Maya's hands in hers and squeezing them. "Maya, it's so good to finally meet you. You, too, Sofia and Gabriella. You look quite stunning in your dresses."

The girls thanked her, but clung to their mother's side. With the travel, the unfamiliar environment and being introduced to new people, he could only imagine how they must feel. He needed to put them at ease.

Liam pointed in the direction of the brown mop of curls and striking blue eyes peeking from behind the sofa. "That handsome chap there is my nephew, Max. He's three and very shy. If we ask him nicely, he might come out and play. What do you think?"

Sofie waved at the little boy as she edged a few steps closer. "Hi, Max. I'm Sofie. This is my little sister, Ella. That's our mommy."

Max stepped from behind the sofa, a wide grin plastered on his face. He wrapped an arm around his uncle's leg and waved a hand in the direction of Ella and Sofie. "Hello."

Maya smiled. "What a handsome young man. It's wonderful to meet you, Max."

He nodded. "Uh-huh."

The adults all laughed. His mother chided him gently. "Sweetie, you're supposed to say it's good to meet you, too."

"What's all this commotion about?" Nigel appeared in the doorway. He looked a bit tired, but he managed a wide smile.

"Father." Liam grinned. "I'd like you to meet Ms. Maya Alvarez and her daughters, Sofia and Gabriella. Ladies, this is my father, Mr. Nigel Westbrook."

"How lovely to finally meet you, my dear." Nigel gave Maya a broad smile as he took her hand in his.

Liam chuckled. The old man was practically smitten. He couldn't blame him. Maya was a gorgeous woman with a smile that would make any man's heart skip a beat.

"Thank you, Mr. Westbrook. It's an honor to finally meet you."

"Nigel, my dear. You must call me Nigel." The old man still appreciated a gorgeous woman. No doubt about that. But he'd have to get his own, because this lovely lady belonged to him: body, heart and soul. And he to her.

Liam handed his niece back to his sister-in-law, then slipped an arm around Maya's waist.

"I need to borrow Maya and the girls for a bit," Liam said.

"For God's sake, man. We've all been dying to meet the woman who has been gracious enough to put up with you," Hunter teased. "You flew her halfway round the world to meet us. No point in trying to keep her from us now. She's bound to discover we're a family of nutters."

Liam punched Hunter in the arm playfully. It felt good to have his brother back. Another reason to be grateful for Maya. Her censure about his inability to forgive his own family had prompted him to do some serious soul-searching. With a bit of prompting, he'd started to mend the fence in his relationship with his brother and Merrie. It felt good to have them in his life again.

The devastation he felt over losing Merrie seemed like a lifetime ago. Now, it was exceedingly clear that they were only meant to be friends. Maya was the woman with whom he was meant to share his life.

And if it was up to him, he'd do just that.

"Fine, but before you all regale her with horrifying tales of the folly of my youth, there's something I need to show her." Liam led Maya and the girls through the French doors and into the heated greenhouse his father had maintained since the death of his mum.

"Is everything okay?" Maya asked.

He squeezed her to him and kissed the top of her head. "Of course, darling. I didn't mean to alarm you, but I want to show you something."

"What?"

"This." Liam waved a hand toward the fragrant pentas, camellias and snowdrops bursting with vibrant color. "This greenhouse was once my mother's pride and joy. We had our best conversations here. When I screwed up, Mum would bring me out here. We'd have tea and chat. She always knew how to get me thinking and back on track."

Liam smiled tightly. So many years had gone by. Still, it hurt like hell that his mum was gone. That she'd been robbed of the opportunity to see her children grow up. Most of all, it hurt that he'd never be able to introduce her to the woman he loved. He blew out a long breath, relieving the sudden pressure in his chest.

"Sometimes, when I really miss her, I come out here, sit and think. I can almost feel her here. I know it sounds crazy—"

"It's not crazy at all. It's beautiful. Sweet." Maya gave him a sad smile and rubbed soothing circles on his back. She was visibly moved. Seemed to feel his hurt and pain as deeply as he did.

He loved this woman. More than he thought possible. Over the past half year she'd been there for him in every way that mattered. She trusted him with her heart and her body. She let him into her life and the lives of her daughters. Gave him a sense of warmth, love and family he hadn't experienced in so very long.

Maybe that was his fault. He'd pushed everyone away. Been afraid. Until Maya.

Beautiful Maya.

She was captivating and strong, like a glittering rare diamond. Gorgeous on the outside and ten times as beautiful deep down, where it counted most.

Lucky bastard.

He didn't deserve her. Didn't deserve the life he'd built with her over the past several months. He'd spent every day trying to be the man she, Sofie and Ella deserved. Not just because it made Maya happy, but because it gave him a soul-deep sense of joy and satisfaction. A feeling that had eluded him his entire life, no matter how great things appeared on the outside.

In this incredible life they were building together, he felt complete.

"Mum was an amazing woman, and she would have adored you." He smiled at Sofie and Ella, who had stooped to smell the flowers. "And she would have spoiled you two rotten."

Maya gave him a smile, then gently laid her hand on his.

"I wish we'd had the chance to get to know her."

"Me, too. I don't know what I've done to deserve you, but you're the love of my life, Maya. I plan to spend the rest of my life proving that to you."

She smiled at him, her eyes wet. "Liam, what are you saying?"

He fingered the blue velvet box buried in his pocket. His heart raced and a light layer of perspiration dampened his back beneath his shirt and suit jacket. He'd been part of cutthroat mergers and tense investor meetings. He'd BASE jumped, skydived, climbed Mount Kilimanjaro. None of those things caused his heart to clench or brought on the sense of panic that now filled his chest. He took her hand and dropped to one knee.

"Before you, I had a nagging emptiness inside that I tried to fill with parties and adventures. I hadn't a clue what was missing from my life until the day I laid eyes on you. I didn't understand what it was just then, but something pulled me to you and refused to let go until I figured it out. What I was missing was you." He fished the box out of his pocket and opened it.

Maya gasped, one hand covering her mouth. Her hand trembled as Liam took it in his and slipped the ring on her left hand. A four-carat, round-cut diamond in a platinum-and-diamond setting that looked like a blooming rose. Three channels of smaller diamonds decorated each side of the band.

The girls were by her side now, their expressions filled with excitement as they looked on.

"Maya Rosita Alvarez, you, Sofie and Ella are the joy of my life. Every day I spend with you is a gift. I never want this to end. So would you please do me the honor of being my wife, and make me the happiest man alive?"

She nodded wildly, tears streaming down her beautiful face. "Yes. Yes! Of course. I love you so much."

The girls jumped up and down, clapping. "Us, too!" Sofie said. Ella echoed her.

Liam stood and kissed Maya, then wrapped them all in a hug. His heart beat so rapidly it felt as if it might burst.

His life was pure perfection. Every crazy, messy bit. Saturday mornings spent coaching the girls' soccer team. Ballet recitals. Picnics at the park. Barbecues with friends. Dinners with family. The quiet moments they spent alone, reading by the fireplace. A life overflowing with unwavering love and consuming desire.

He didn't want it any other way.

* * * * *

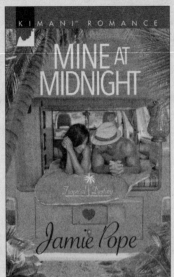

SPECIAL EXCERPT FROM

⒣ HARLEQUIN®

KIMANI
ROMANCE

An ambitious daughter of a close-knit Louisiana clan,
Kamaya Boudreaux is making a name for herself in the
business world. But when her secret venture is threatened
to be exposed, she needs to do some serious damage
control. Her plans don't include giving in to temptation
with her sexy business partner, Wesley Walters...

Read on for a sneak peek at
A PLEASING TEMPTATION, the next exciting
installment in author Deborah Fletcher Mello's
***THE BOUDREAUX FAMILY** series!*

Wesley reached into the briefcase that rested beside his
chair leg. He passed her the folder of documents. "They're
all signed," he said as he extended his hand to shake hers.
"I look forward to working with you, Kamaya Boudreaux."

She slid her palm against his, the warmth of his touch
heating her spirit. "Same here, Wesley Walters. I imagine
we're going to make a formidable team."

"Team! I like that."

"You should. Because it's so out of character for me! I
don't usually play well with others."

He chuckled. "Then I'm glad you chose me to play
with first."

A cup of coffee and a few questions kept Kamaya and Wesley talking for almost three hours. After sharing more than either had planned, they stood, saying their goodbyes and making plans to see each other again.

"I would really love to take you to dinner," Wesley said as he walked Kamaya to her car.

"Are you asking me out on a date, Wesley Walters?"

He grinned. "I am. With one condition."

"What's that?"

"We don't talk business. I get the impression that's not an easy thing for you to do. So will you accept the challenge?"

As they reached her car, she smiled as she nodded her head. "I'd love to."

"I mean it about not talking business."

Kamaya laughed. "You really don't know me."

He laughed with her. "I don't, but I definitely look forward to changing that."

Wesley opened the door of her vehicle. The air between them was thick and heavy, carnal energy sweeping from one to the other, fervent with desire. It was intense and unexpected, and left them both feeling a little awkward and definitely excited about what might come.

"Drive safely, Kamaya," he whispered softly, watching as she slid into the driver's seat.

She nodded. "You, too, Wesley. Have a really good night."

Don't miss A PLEASING TEMPTATION
by Deborah Fletcher Mello, available April 2017
wherever Harlequin® Kimani Romance™
books and ebooks are sold.